TO KILL AN

ERROR

Jed B. van de Poll was born in 1956 and grew up in Derbyshire. He lives in Dublin, Ireland with his wife Pamela. *To Kill an Error* is his first book.

TO KILL AN
ERROR

Jed B. van de Poll

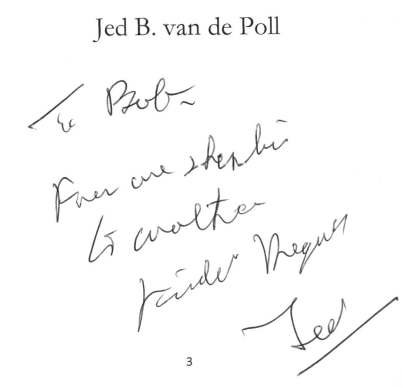

ISBN-13: 978-1484137444
ISBN-10: 1484137442

To Kill an Error
Jed B. van de Poll

Contents

To Tess, without whom this book would
never have seen the light of day

Seth could feel the downdraft of the rotor blades; he could just about make out the reed beds on the bank through the retreating fog. It felt like a scene from a National Geographic documentary, the caribou trying to cross the mud flats to get away from the hunters, eventually grinding to a halt, mud up to its belly caught in the cross hairs of the marksman, but in Seth's case, he did not think his hunters were packing tranquiliser darts – something more lethal, no doubt. But he didn't care. He was utterly exhausted, his energy levels so low he did not have the strength to lift even one foot out of the clawing mud, sucking at his calves. All his senses were overwhelmed by the cold, the fog and the deafening noise of those damned rotor blades. Why didn't they get on with it?

PART I

Few challenges facing America – and the world – are more urgent than combating climate change. The science is beyond dispute and the facts are clear. Sea levels are rising. Coastlines are shrinking. We've seen record drought, spreading famine, and storms that are growing stronger with each passing hurricane season. Climate change ... if left unaddressed, will continue to weaken our economy and threaten our national security.

Barack Obama,

18 November 2008

Ben Haze looked at the newscast. He had done it. Not all of the states were in but the results were now clearly beyond doubt. The environmental movement had their man in the Whitehouse, and it was he, Ex-Vice President Ben Haze, who had put him there.

He had been so close himself all those years ago. How could he forget the stolen election? It should have been him in the Oval Office, but the Democrats had been kept out for eight long years, which had in turn put back the cause of combatting global warming.

Susan Fletcher had been the obvious frontrunner for the Democrat nomination, which would have guaranteed her the Presidency. A Democratic landslide was inevitable after eight years of mismanagement by the GOP, but she did not understand the importance of the whole environmental movement and its potential impact on the world. Neither had she been interested in the colossal personal gain that could be obtained from the right investments at the right time, especially when, as the POTUS, one could influence the legislature to divert the vast resources at the disposal of an American President to further particular aims. Fletcher's contempt for the Greens had cost her dear. She had run out of campaign funds at a critical stage and an unknown lawyer from Boston had pipped her at the post – with a little help from his friends.

It had been Senator Mecheri's good fortune to bump into Ben Haze at a global warming fundraiser in 2002, which had led to their joint investment in the Boston Carbon Exchange (BCX), Haze through his General Incorporated Mutual Company and Mecheri through funding from the Fitzpatrick Endowment. In fact, it was the funding from this foundation that helped to launch the BCX, in no small part due to Mecheri's seat on the Endowment's Board of Directors.

This close association between Mecheri and one of the Democratic Party's grandees had been the springboard for the election of the first United States President of Asian descent. But it was more than just the patronage of an ex-Vice President that had secured the White House for Mecheri; it was the vast resources of a worldwide environmental movement that foresaw the potential of having one of their own as the most powerful individual on the planet.

The received wisdom was that the President had been propelled into office by funding for his campaign from millions of small donations, much of it pledged through judicious use of social media and online campaigning. In fact, the big money had come from outside the United States, using back channels that funnelled large donations from influential individuals on the global environmental scene.

Mecheri's election was the final link in the chain. The President was planning to appoint his own men to key places, such as Jiang Yat-sen as his Science Tsar — an old college room-mate and now a respected Stanford professor. As a result Haze was able to push ahead with changes to environmental legislation. These changes would, he hoped, make him the first environmental billionaire via his investment in the BCX. And after Mecheri had served his second term, Haze would be ideally placed for a second run at the Presidency. With his personal wealth and the support of the Greens, not just in the United States but throughout the world, he would not fail again.

CHAPTER 1

S eth Whitten had been brought up in a family steeped in the ethos of green living. Weekends spent disrupting fox hunts; daily trips to the compost heap with potato peelings; twice yearly night-time vigils to 'help a toad across the road', long cycles to school, not just to save the bus fare but to save the world too. He could think of no better way to help the planet than to put his brain to work on the problem directly.

After a degree in Computer Science Seth was no different from many hundreds of his compatriots when it came to deciding on postgraduate studies – he followed the money. This led him to Norwich, in the heart of the English countryside, for a Masters in Climate Change at the government-funded Page Climate Centre.

His particular area of interest was temperature mapping so he could make use of his IT skills when applying temperature data to computer models of future global warming. This was postgrad heaven; to study at one of the best-funded research units in the world and to rub shoulders with some of the greats in climate change research, such as Joe Sharkey and Lance Corbin. These people ate, drank and slept environmental science. Not only that, they practised what they preached. They cycled, they recycled, they knew their carbon footprint and they planted trees when there was no alternative to air travel; he had come home.

It was spring 2010, one of those dank dismal fenland days that you get in East Anglia. The British Meteorological Office had forecast a beautiful day but instead torrential rain had cancelled his picnic with the lovely Connie.

Once again Seth was stuck indoors. He had been looking forward to the picnic, but now Connie wanted to finish an essay instead. All he had to do was trawl the myriad wackjob global warming sceptic websites that proliferated on the Internet. Their ignorant, ill-informed rants enraged him.

So the sceptics think our climate models are bunkum, do they? OK, that's an easy one to counter. As my old professor at Cambridge used to say, 'Seth, ma' boy, predictive power is the test of a theory, remember that – predictive power.'

Then let's apply our theories to the past. Let's crunch the numbers of the last 350 years of weather data for the UK. Let's predict climate in 1710, the temperature in Greenwich in 1810 and in the Britain of 1910. We already know the results so we can prove how accurate our models really are.

Now this was no small undertaking. For the exercise to have any validity at all, the data sets would have to be accurate, checked and double-checked.

He launched into the task with alacrity. When

he wasn't in the arms of Connie, this was his idea of a fun time!

* * * * *

It had been weeks now. Seth had checked and double-checked: this made no sense. All the predictions were way out. Temperatures by 2010 should have been 6°C higher than they were. The sea levels had risen but then sea levels had been rising for the last 13,000 years, since the end of the last ice age. In fact, they had risen 120m but that equated to less than 10mm per year, not the 10cm per year predicted by the models. It was no wonder then that when the model's predictions were extrapolated over the next 50 years to 2060; they came up with the enormous sea level rises that the Page Climate Centre had been predicting.

He ran the simulation again. There was something eerily familiar about the shape of the graphs he was getting. A few years back there had been a bit of a brouhaha about a world temperature graph produced by an American professor, Nigel Nevin, from Colorado University. The graph had become the poster child of the global warming movement, showing that world temperatures had remained static for the last 1,500 years, until the start of the Industrial Revolution when they had suddenly taken a sharp leap skywards.

All was peachy until some statisticians applied themselves to the formula used, raising serious questions about its validity. The graph then became the subject of huge division in the climatological world pitching colleague against colleague but eventually it faded from the headlines and was deftly swept under the global warming carpet.

Now the results that Seth was getting smacked of the same 'anomaly'. There seemed to be a tendency for the climate modelling software to predict excessive rises, whether it was in temperature or sea level. This had also been a feature of the so-called 'Nevin' graph. Could there be a link?

This gave him an idea. One of the less savoury things that Seth had indulged in as a somewhat wayward undergraduate at Cambridge was hacking the college computers and changing the grades of 'friends in need'. He now decided to put his talents, honed over many years, to a more clandestine and equally career-threatening use. Could there be a link between the Nevin graph and the strange results he was getting from his simulations? Maybe a look at the departmental staff's email accounts would give him a lead?

But before he could begin his trawl a mail dropped into his own account, summoning him to a meeting with none other than Professor Joe Sharkey – head of Page Climate Centre. Seth gathered up his notepad and headed over to the admin. block. This was a first for him, a lowly postgrad, being called to the hallowed halls of Joe Sharkey's office.

Sharkey was a legend among the glitterati of the environmental movement. Seth had researched the life of his hero before joining Norwich University. His formulae for calculating the average world temperature were an academic yardstick.

Seth's mind was racing. What had the Prof. in mind? Was it some special project that Sharkey wanted him to work on or had one of his lecturers singled him out for special mention. *Any chance of a Doctoral scholarship, Joe?*

On entering Sharkey's office Seth realised he had been a tad optimistic. The professor was purple with rage. What did Seth think he was doing running unauthorised programs on the university's supercomputer? Who had given him permission to spend time formulating infantile algorithms to test HIS data? If Seth wanted to remain at the college to get a Masters he had better start knuckling down to what was on the course curriculum and leave the real research to those who knew what they were doing…

'Now get out.'

From entering the office to leaving it, Seth spoke not a word. He was gobsmacked. He wandered in a daze over to the cafeteria, trying to gather his thoughts and make sense of what had just happened. There was no ban on supercomputer time for postgrads. You submitted your program and data and it was run when time was available. Theoretically you needed permission from your tutor, but in reality, nobody bothered and certainly no one he knew had ever been hauled over the coals for such a minor infraction of the rules.

What had gotten into Sharkey? Clearly Seth had crossed some line and any chance of him getting a First had gone to sleep with the fishes. He held his mug of coffee with both hands trying to get some comfort out of the lukewarm brew. Sweet Jesus, what had he done?

Whatever it was, it had to be something to do with the fact that the historical temperature data did not stack up when compared with the climate model predictions. He had definitely touched a raw nerve here with Sharkey and being warned off made Seth even more determined to find a possible link with Nevin.

That evening he logged onto the college mail server after he confirmed that Sharkey had left the building. Just to be on the safe side, he had checked Sharkey's parking space to make sure the green Prius was gone. The Prof's password was easy to guess, GAIA, one of the primordial gods, the so called 'Earth Mother' of Greek mythology. Like Hitler's birthday – which could have opened half the safes in Nazi Germany – Gaia would get you into half the email accounts of those in the green movement.

Seth was interested in any communication between the disgraced Nigel Nevin and Page Climate Centre. Fortunately, Sharkey was an untidy fellow and appeared to have done little or no housekeeping on his email account since it had been set up. Every email he had ever received or sent seemed to be still on the server. But Seth did not have time to wade through this mass of data, so he ran a search on Nevin. Bingo! Either Sharkey was having an affair with this guy or they had an awful lot to discuss on a daily basis. With no time to lose, Seth dumped the contents of the folders onto his pocket hard drive. Who else might be involved? Basically any of the top brass at Page. Seth set about hacking the accounts of all the departmental staff – the Earth goddess making his task that much easier.

One mail jumped out at him, it was from Professor Joe Sharkey to Steve, Nigel, and Norman and dated October 2009 –

> Hi guys,
>
> Concerned with latest global temperature figures. The plateau we are having to admit to is bad enough so I've just completed Nigel's data trick by substituting in the real temps from Lance's satellite records from 1979 to date to hide the decline in the proxy series.
>
> Thanks to you all for getting back with your comments.
>
> Kind regards
>
> Joe
>
> Professor Joseph Sharkey

What the hell? This mail from Sharkey was to the two originators of the infamous Nevin graph – Stephen Cotterall and Nigel Nevin. The Lance referred to was none other than Seth's own lecturer, Dr Lance Corbin. This gave him another line of enquiry for his email research.

Seth ran a quick Google search on one of the better-informed sceptic websites which, he recalled, had conducted a critique of Nevin's graph.

According to thesepticsceptic.com, what Nevin had done was fairly simple. Using approximate temperature data from very old trees such as the bristle cone pine, he had established a correlation between the tree ring growth and global temperatures. Applying his own special algorithm, Nevin produced an approximation of the world's temperature over the last 1,500 years.

The sceptics' problem with the graph, which showed correlating temperature increase from the beginning of the industrial age in step with the increase in carbon dioxide concentration in the atmosphere, was that after 1979, the tree ring data showed world temperatures *declining*, not increasing, as actual temperature measurements were showing. It seems this was the 'trick' referred to in the email – simply abandon the proxy tree ring data and use thermometer-based data in parts where it suited the desired outcome: increasing temperatures. This was the point at which the sceptics cried foul, maintaining that the apparent correlation for the previous 1,500 years had simply been a coincidence, as subsequent analysis of his data would show.

Sceptic rants had never bothered Seth much before. What was worrying about this explanation was that Prof. Joe Sharkey *et al* knew what Nevin had done and were employing the same tactic to get their own research to show what they wanted.

Seth decided to do more checks on the Page Climate Centre's other studies and some in-depth statistical analysis of the vast amount of temperature data that the organisation held in its data banks. For that he needed access to a supercomputer and Sharkey had just barred him from the one at Norwich University.

The college had two Cray XT5 'jaguar' supercomputers funded by grants from the very green New Labour government. They were known as the Kray Twins (why, he did not know, no doubt some sort of intellectual in-joke). But as he no longer had access, he turned to his good friend Ali Djalili at the Samsung University in Seoul. They had a Cray XT7. Maybe he could blag some time on this 4 petaflop monster. Ali owed him one for a slight manipulation of results during their days together at Cambridge. He was calling in the marker.

Djalili acceded to his request and provided access to the Cray, so long as Seth used it only through the hours of Korean darkness, which fortunately coincided with Seth's daytime, Seoul being eight hours ahead. He began to stream the Climate Centre data over to Korea on a gigabit link during English night when the network was lightly used and then crunch the numbers on the Cray during the English day. The process took several days but early on, it became clear what Nevin, Sharkey and Corbin were up to. After several weeks of going through the figures, Seth was sure he was right about what he had discovered.

A basic statistical analysis of their work showed clear cherry picking of the figures. If a particular temperature reading did not meet the criteria, then it was deemed to be aberrant and therefore dropped from the data set. There seemed to be only two forms of data kept by Page, raw and cooked. The raw data was heavily protected, buried in the bowels of the college.

It was this data that Sharkey appeared to be trying to conceal. Seth's innocent trawling of the previous few weeks had obviously triggered some sort of flag in the system alerting Sharkey's security to unauthorised delving into the real data. But what was going on here? Why would Nevin, Sharkey and Corbin take such risks with their professional careers? Surely it couldn't be just to further the ends of the green movement?

There had to be more to it than simple left-wing political thinking. Seth went back to ploughing through the copious e-mails to and from Joe Sharkey. An unusual name caught his attention, Professor Jiang Yat-sen of Stanford University. He decided to follow the email thread but, to his astonishment, he discovered that both professors were using PGP (Pretty Good Protection), a very sophisticated form of encryption.

The problem was how to get around this security because he was not going to crack the cypher anytime this side of the second coming, even with the use of Ali's Cray 7. What he needed to do to read the messages between Yat-sen and Sharkey was to steal two keys. But these were not any ordinary keys; these were electronic pieces of code, 1s and 0s.

Sharkey's should not be too difficult. If Seth could gain access to his office, he could simply break into his computer and copy the key onto a memory stick. Yat-sen would be a different kettle of fish. Without Yat-sen's private key, he would be able to read messages from Yat-sen to Sharkey, but not from Sharkey to Yat-sen – this encryption was good. But how to access Sharkey's office without being caught? He needed to figure out a plan to both circumvent the locks and the video surveillance. A smile flickered across his face as the solutions began to present themselves.

* * * * *

Seth hung back on the Friday night, once again making sure that Sharkey's Prius was gone. He knew that any attempt to enter the office through the door would alert security – he did not want to arouse suspicion. He would go around the door or, as it were, over it.

Like everywhere else in the university, people paid lip service to security. The offices were cheaply built and while the doors had very expensive proximity keyless locks, the interior walls did not go all the way up to the next floor. A panelled false ceiling sat on top of the walls, leaving a crawl space above all of the offices and corridors through which cabling, pipes, etc. were run and could be easily accessed. It would be equally easy to climb up through a panel in the corridor ceiling, along the crawl space and down through a panel in Sharkey's office, and this, with consummate ease, is what Seth did.

Once in Sharkey's office, Seth's heart began to race. It was one thing to hack into someone's computer from some remote location, well shielded from any prying eyes; it was another to be physically standing in front of your boss's computer, putting your future career on the line. Seth approached the PC monitor from behind. If Sharkey had any sense of security at all, he would have time-lapse software operating his webcam, taking a frame every few seconds of whoever was sitting at the keyboard. This could then be tied back to any activity on the computer to establish who had been doing what and when.

Seth set about attaching a 10cm long rod to the base of the camera. At the end of the rod at right angles to the camera was a small photograph of an office wall. Not identical to this office but close as made no difference. It was only after this precaution was in place that Seth dared to move around to the front of the desk, neatly shielded from the webcam by his Heath Robinson contraption. While this simple device would not convince under close scrutiny of the video, together with the little software patch he was going to run to erase all evidence of any keystrokes on the computer, it made him confident that no one would be looking for anything suspicious in the first place.

Plugging a memory stick into the small USB hub on Sharkey's desk, Seth switched on the monitor. To his surprise, Sharkey had not even bothered to enable the basic screen password protection on his computer. Perhaps the false sense of security provided by the high tech lock on the door had led to this lapse; either way this was a bonus for Seth, saving him a few minutes hacking the password. Once into the PGP folder, he copied Sharkey's private key onto the memory stick – job done.

But then Seth realised he didn't need Yat-sen's private key: all the original e-mails from Sharkey to Yat-sen were here on Sharkey's computer – pre-encryption. All he needed to do was dump Sharkey's Outlook 'sent items' onto the stick and scarper. This process, together with any archived items, he swiftly accomplished and Seth was soon back up in the crawl space about to make a drop down into the corridor. In his excitement at getting all of Sharkey's e-mails, he realised he had forgotten to remove the photo frame from Sharkey's webcam.

'Damn it!'

He had begun to replace the corridor ceiling tile he had just lifted when he spotted one of Sharkey's postgrads walking down the corridor towards him. He allowed the tile to noiselessly settle back into place and held his breath. The student swiped a fob over the door lock and entered Sharkey's office. That was it! It would be obvious someone had been tampering with Sharkey's computer and the hunt would be on for the culprit. After the row with the Professor the previous day, Seth reckoned that he would be at the top of the list. He was toast. Not only had he forgotten to remove the photo frame, he had forgotten to run the keystroke deletion subroutine – he was definitely not cut out for this cloak and dagger malarkey.

But almost as quickly as the student had entered Sharkey's office, he left it. Seth gingerly lifted the ceiling tile on the office side of the corridor wall and there on the desk was a folder marked for Sharkey's attention. The student had just dumped the file and walked out. The novice spy had been given a second chance and he was not going to blow it. Dropping back down into the office, Seth replaced the memory stick in the machine and ran the keystroke deletion code. Moving behind the monitor, he quickly removed the photo frame and made his escape through the ceiling.

Back at his apartment, Seth collapsed on his bed and waited for the stress to leave his body. His heartbeat was still over 100 and his ears were ringing like a bell. His clothes were drenched in sweat and his hands would not stop shaking. He could not go through that again; he simply was not built for espionage.

As he began to relax, the enormity of what he was getting himself into began to dawn. If he carried on down this path, there was no going back. There were only two outcomes – the end of his academic career, with possible gaol time, or the exposure of Professor Sharkey and his data manipulation. And at this point, his trembling hands were telling him that the former was the more likely. He needed to clear his head.

He showered and put on his cycling togs and headed out of Fernley House and off to do a lap of the park, a nice 5 K round trip. Out of the campus and onto the prettily named Cowslip Road, tree-lined and seemingly rural, with the lake on one side and the park on the other. His mind began to clear. There was a lot of grunt work to be done, sifting through the myriad e-mails looking for dirt and examining the computer code, scanning for errors deliberate or otherwise. He was going to need help; he could not do this on his own. The dilemma: to involve Connie in his crusade and possibly put her in danger, or to involve one of the other postgrads and risk betrayal.

There was no one he trusted like Connie – the decision was made.

CHAPTER 2

Seth was exasperated.

'But can't you see it's the worst sort of scientific malpractice – straight up honest to goodness data fraud,'

Connie had not taken the revelation well.

'Maybe there's some other explanation. Maybe you're misreading the data – they can't all be crooks.'

Ever the one to see good in everyone, Connie was not going to be persuaded by mere words – it was going to take hard evidence and persistence, not unlike his first attempts to woo her.

'Take a look at this.'

He showed her the email from Joe Sharkey to Nigel Nevin.

'You can see that Nevin is a data twister and Sharkey goes along with it. It's there in black and white – he is trying to "hide the decline". He knows temperatures are falling and he is deliberately trying to show that they aren't. What more evidence do you want – his confession written in blood?'

Seth needed her on his side, someone to tell him he was right, not a doubting Thomasina.

'Calm down, calm down, you are going to burst a blood vessel if you go on like this. Yes, I get it. You think Sharkey and his associates are manipulating temperature readings to fit their projections but what can we do about it? I'm sure many academics take such liberties, although I grant you this seems a bit extreme.'

'But there is more to this than just data manipulation. I think Yat-sen is also implicated.'

Now Seth was losing her. 'Who's this Yat-sen character? Sounds like someone out of a Jackie Chan movie.'

'He's a Stanford lecturer. He's why I need you; I have found encrypted e-mails on Sharkey's computer between himself and Yat-sen. I can't do this by myself. I need someone I can trust to split the task and start going through the correspondence to see if they're hiding anything else. Connie, like Darwin said, I need to kill the error – will you help me?'

Seth related the details of his meeting with Sharkey and how he balled him out for using computer time to research the archived temperature records at the Page Climate Centre.

'This is serious, Seth. Sharkey will have his eye on you. If anything leaks out about dodgy temperature records or the like, you are going to be his first port of call. Promise me you won't do anything dangerous.'

'I promise.'

'Really?'

'Yes. Cross my heart…'

'OK. In that case, I will help you. Show me what you need to do and we can work out some way of dividing up the task.'

'Well, the first thing we need to do is to go through the encrypted email traffic between Sharkey and Yat-sen. I think this will be the most revealing and also nowhere near as much work as trawling through the main email database. Perhaps we will get lucky and find clues to other members of the faculty who are involved in hiding data.'

Returning to Fernley House, Seth and Connie sat down and divided the email file between Seth's desktop computer and Connie's notebook. They lapsed into silence as they waded through banalities of correspondence between two self-opinionated professors discussing the finer points of environmental research. This was not looking promising. The nature of the encrypted files seemed to differ little from the simply password-controlled e-mails Seth had hacked off the server. Why were Sharkey and Yat-sen so scared of anyone reading these particular mails? The discussion seemed to centre on the establishment of the Boston Carbon Trading Exchange in 2003.

'Look at this here. They're saying that a carbon trading exchange was a prerequisite for the taxing of carbon emissions produced by industry on a worldwide basis. The BCX would enable the big polluters like the coal, oil and steel industries to start trading carbon credits with the rest of the world – particularly developing nations who were to be given enormous carbon credits by the UN for not cutting down rainforests or not building coal-fired power stations. The idea seems to be that the money that they raised by selling these carbon credits on the open market could then be used to install renewable energy power grids in their countries. This would enable them to afford to undertake a low – or preferably, no carbon – industrial revolution.'

Connie took it in. 'But that's good right?'

'Yes, but in reality, all that happens is that the money goes into the coffers of the ruling kleptocrats and the poor nations stay poor. Having said that, the West feels virtuous in knowing that it has offset carbon emissions and transferred some of the vast wealth of the industrialised world to some of the poorer nations on the planet.'

But why were Sharkey and Yat-sen so excited about it? It was a side show. Many other exchanges had subsequently opened up in London, Sydney, Frankfurt and New York. The BCX did not have a monopoly on carbon trading and, so far as Seth knew, neither Sharkey nor Yat-sen had any interest in carbon trading. Like most other things in this world, Seth was convinced it came down to money.

According to the e-mails, one individual was central to the establishment of the BCX. He seemed to be some sort of hot shot politico but he was never referred to by name. He was known as 'the Puppet Master'. He appeared to be on track for high political office and would be the environmental movement's man on the inside, guiding the industrial giant that was the United States in the right environmental direction. What had happened to him, Seth did not know. There was no one in the Mecheri administration that he knew of that fitted the description. But from the tenor of the e-mails, this man was obviously key.

* * * * *

In spite of his promise to Connie, Seth couldn't resist leaking some of the juicier e-mails between Sharkey and various global warming big wigs; he particularly liked Sharkey's description of an astro-physicist on the climate sceptic wing of the argument as 'an arrogant asshole'. There was some-thing so satisfying about the spectacle of one academic slagging off another, like two naughty schoolboys in the playground. This puerile behav-iour had stripped away the gloss of respectability and, yes, superiority that seemed to attach to senior members of academia. While this email merely showed the contempt that each side in the debate had for each other, Seth hoped that it would draw people in to read the 'nature trick' email and under-stand what they were doing – the flagrant manipulation of the world's temperature data by a coterie of highly paid 'university types'.

But as with any good thriller, the protagonists needed to have motive for their skulduggery to intrigue and outrage the public. This was the diffi-cult bit. Grant aid and government sponsorship, research funding and renewable energy subsidies did not set the heart a-flutter. Academics had been falsifying their research since the inception of the scientific method. If the data didn't fit, scientists would make it fit, or out would go the hand for more research money to establish why the data did not fit.

There had been a time when all the doctor or the professor had to do was publish. Get five or six articles a year into some learned journal, write the odd book – this would be enough to maintain their stature and, most importantly their tenure, at an institute of their choice. But times had changed; there was now an onus to bring in research grant money for the college. The pressures were enormous, and therefore the expectation that a researcher would come up with the results that their paymasters wanted was even greater – whatever the data said.

But who were the paymasters? On the surface it appeared to be the governments of the world, with no purer motives than clean energy and a pollution-free environment. Who could argue with that? But scratch below the surface and one might begin to see different motives. And this is where Seth made his mistake. He published an apparently innocuous email from Joe Sharkey to a board of enquiry at Stanford in support of Professor Jiang Yat-sen in his defence against accusations of misappropriating grant aid. By leaking this email Seth had wanted to show a link between Sharkey and Yat-sen.

This was a big mistake; there was a veritable

shit storm. Norwich University went into overdrive to find out who had leaked the e-mails. All the academic staff were called in by Sharkey. He wanted names of possible suspects; he wanted the students' data stores (all 18,000 of them) searched for evidence of hacking. He demanded interviews with anyone who could have had access to the university's email servers – and of course he wanted to see Seth.

CHAPTER 3

'We have a problem, Joseph.'

Yat-sen's call both surprised and alarmed Sharkey. He was not in the habit of phoning Page. Early on in their relationship they had both agreed that it would not look too good in the British press if it were known that a British government research unit was receiving money from the Chinese government, no matter how innocent the reason.

'Have you seen the *Guardian* this morning, Joseph?'

Yat-sen had long been a fan of the English left-leaning newspaper. He was referring to an article headlined 'Climategate' that published the email on 'hiding the decline' that Seth had leaked to the web.

'You have a mole, my friend. We need to find him and quickly. We need to know what he knows – how deeply he has penetrated; then we will need to mend some fences with my government associates in China. They will not be pleased.'

Sharkey took the hint. The forensic team arrived that afternoon. They were a private organisation, specialising in computer, as well as medical, forensics. Four men and one woman descended on his office, three analysing his computer while the other two hoovered his keyboard and desk. Having gathered all the material, they returned to London and began the painstaking task of reviewing the watchdog time-lapse frames from Sharkey's webcam and building a DNA database from the dust on the desk and in the keyboard to be compared with the DNA samples obtained from suspects at a later date.

* * * * *

As soon as Connie heard about the leaked email, she had gone ballistic. Seth tried to persuade her that putting the e-mails into the public domain had been the right thing to do. However, he was now exposed. If only he had kept Yat-sen out of it, he might have been able to continue digging in peace, but he was too impatient to point the finger. He still had thousands of e-mails to go through and as yet he could not get a firm handle on why Yat-sen was being so generous in channelling Chinese government funding Sharkey's way.

The prospect of the interview had given him nightmares. Sharkey had conducted it personally, one of many he had held that week. Seth kept reminding himself that they were just fishing. If they had anything on him, he would either be in gaol or out on his ear. He had to stay calm, not give anything away. When he entered Sharkey's office, the Professor appeared relaxed. This had been the fifth interview that day and Sharkey had his routine off pat. He offered Seth a chair and a coffee and asked a series of prepared questions.

Had Seth ever hacked the university computers?

Did he know of anyone who had hacked the computers?

Had he any suspicions about who might have leaked the university's e-mails?

Blaah blaah blaah. It was like a scene from the McCarthy witch hunts, but in the end the interrogation had been surprisingly non-taxing. Seth left the office on a high. Clearly the Professor had no suspicions. Sharkey was just going through the motions.

As the door of the office closed behind the departing student, Sharkey got up from his chair, walked over to the recycle bin and, with the tweezers provided, retrieved the empty coffee cup. He carefully placed it in a plastic Ziploc bag. He consulted a list on his computer then wrote a 5 digit reference number on the pouch and dropped it into the box under his desk for collection by Forensics.

* * * * *

Inspector Franks sighed. It was going to be a long night. The examination of Sharkey's office had been meticulous.

'Now, show me what you've got.'

Franks was reviewing the accumulated data from days of interviews and clandestine snooping. While ostensibly an officer working for the Metropolitan Police, she did a nice side line in undercover forensics for whoever would pay her. Trying to make ends meet on an Inspector's salary, even with London weighting, was a fool's game. This particular type of business was right up her street. A bit of private detective work – using some of Her Majesty's diagnostic equipment courtesy of the taxpayer – nothing too illegal and the client was a very good payer.

She had already established a DNA match with one of the cups and a skin flake vacuumed from the Professor's keyboard. The reference number on the evidence bag, 87932, corresponded to a cup handled by one Joan Weston. She was not very high on the list of suspects and did not have the necessary profile for a computer hacker. What was intriguing, though, was what the forensic computer analyst was now showing Franks from the 'Watchdog' feed. It occurred just eight days previously. Running the video as a stream rather than individual frames meant that weeks of time-lapse photography could be processed in a matter of hours.

What had caught the analyst's eye were just 10 frames representing five minutes of real time. Initially all that Franks could see was just a mottled blue and white wall, common to many offices on Sharkey's floor, intermittently interspersed with the face of the Professor sitting at his computer. But for those 10 frames, the wall suddenly came into sharp relief as though the camera had changed focus for a few minutes. This was not possible, as it was a low quality, fixed focus webcam, incapable of such an operation. The frames were lifted and placed in a blink comparator, alternately flashing the frame prior to the change and after the change. Someone had placed a picture of the wall in front of the camera for five minutes and then removed it. It must have been within a few inches of the camera, which accounted for the sharp focus and was the only reason the perpetrator's deception had been noticed.

The hacker probably thought that no one would look and had not bothered to adjust the clarity of the photograph – fortunately for Franks, not so fortunate for the hacker. This gave the inspector an exact time at which Sharkey's computer had been interfered with. This in turn enabled the analysts to zone in on any anomalies that might have occurred during that five-minute window, and it was this final discovery that showed what a sophisticated hack they were dealing with.

A program had been run that deleted the keystrokes made during the attack. This did not remove the evidence of the copying of Sharkey's inbox and outbox. But here it got really interesting. A select group of e-mails, both in and out, had been deleted. The deletion was very crude and had been conducted over a week after the original hack. The majority of the e-mails were recoverable but it was not possible to read them as they were encrypted and used a public private key method that made them to all intents and purposes uncrackable. The deletion of these emails was beyond Franks' remit but she was curious.

'Pull me up the 'Watchdog' frames for the half hour around when the encrypted e-mails were deleted.'

The analyst's fingers whirred over the keyboard and presented the relevant section. Franks dismissed him from the room while she perused the video. She had an uncontrollable urge to laugh out loud; she smothered it with a loud choking cough.

'Is everything alright, Ma'am?' the analyst enquired from behind the door.

'Yes, sorry, coffee went down the wrong way,' she managed to splutter.

Professor Sharkey was clearly out of his depth when it came to any sort of technology. There he sat, head jerking around like some half-crazed automaton, as the time-lapse frames rolled by. Nothing strange there, but what cracked her up was that there was a two-minute gap in the recording where the 'Watchdog' had been switched off while Sharkey himself must have deleted the encrypted e-mails. It had not dawned on him that he was visible either side of the recording and that there was only one person who could have made the deletions. God help the planet if this buffoon was the one in charge of measuring its temperature.

She called the analyst back in and instructed him to delete the entire day's 'Watchdog' recording and remove any reference in his own logs. There was no point in embarrassing her paymaster, but she was still intrigued as to why he felt it so important to remove evidence of these particular e-mails, even from her prying eyes.

There still remained the matter of who had conducted the original hack. She was being paid a lot of money to conduct this investigation and its primary goal was the identification of the perp. Her reputation and future earnings depended on finding out who had done this. Suspect number 87932, Ms Weston, was apparently an unlikely suspect for the hack, but maybe she was involved in some other way, as support or maybe she was the one who placed the photo in front of the webcam. Franks decided to call her in for questioning.

* * * * *

This was a delicate operation for Franks. She was not conducting the interview in an official capacity; she did not want to draw attention to herself and she particularly did not want anyone asking questions about her afterwards, so going in hard and trying to break down 87932 was not a runner. Low key and subtle was the way to play this. Weston was a small mousey woman, no makeup, canvas shoes and a faint whiff of body odour. From her file, Franks could see she had a PhD in Environmental Science and lectured at the college – pity the poor students on a hot summer's day with this one.

Franks played it very deferential. As it was lunch time, she had ordered in ham sandwiches and coffee and began by offering her interviewee a bite to eat. An offer of a root up the arse with a red hot poker could not have gone down worse.

'I am a vegan, Inspector. Thanks but no thanks.'

'Sorry, sorry, Dr Weston, I did not realise.'

Franks called her assistant and had the platter taken away.

'A cup of coffee, perhaps?'

'No, just a glass of tap water, if you don't mind.'

What a disaster. Franks was so on the back foot and more than ever convinced that this woman had nothing to do with the hack, but DNA does not lie.

'As you may know, the college is investigating the theft of certain information from the offices of Professor Sharkey and the college computers.'

'Yes yes, a dreadful business. Poor Joseph. He has been traumatised by the whole affair. The publicity has begun to affect his health, poor dear. I do hope you find who did this. Anything I can do to help – just ask.'

'Well I believe that there may be a way for you to help me. We are trying to eliminate as many people from our inquiries as we can. We want to establish where everyone who had access to Professor Sharkey's office was on the day of the theft, to narrow our search. Did you by any chance have any reason to use the Professor's computer in the last month?'

'You don't think that I had anything to do with this, do you?' The woman looked genuinely affronted.

'No, no, I am in no way suggesting such a thing. It is just that we have to cover all possibilities and knowing who has been in his office would be very helpful.'

'Well, it wasn't me who touched his computer. I was in Joseph's office yesterday when he kindly invited me in for a chat but this was the first time I had seen him in over two months, as I am only just back from a lecture tour of the United States.'

Franks couldn't get her out of the office fast enough. What the hell was Forensics playing at? This woman wasn't even in the country when Sharkey's computer was hacked. She needed to go back to basics. How could the good doctor's DNA have possibly got onto Sharkey's keyboard? Franks took another look at the evidence. She pulled out the cup from its plastic bag. Something was not right. Had there been cross-contamination? Could one of the technicians have touched the keyboard and then this cup? No way. These guys were professionals; this was their speciality – they were not going to make such a fundamental mistake. It had to be something else.

Then it hit her – the smell. There was a brown residue at the bottom of the cup and, when held to the nose, an unmistakable aroma of coffee. Dr Weston, God bless her, only drank tap water. This could not possibly be her cup; therefore it was not her DNA.

'Bring me the bin from the interview room,' Franks barked down the phone.

A flustered and somewhat bemused secretary entered with the bin, which Franks proceeded to empty out onto the desk. There were several plastic cups but only two without lipstick on them. Franks was a prodigious consumer of coffee. Of the two remaining, one was coffee-stained and the other was not. It had only ever contained, water, tap water.

'Get me the DNA off this cup and match it against sample 87932, and don't fuck it up this time.'

Franks was incandescent with rage. They had lost at least 24 hours farting around with the false lead. Professionals? They were a bunch of peons. An hour later, the two DNA traces were on the desk, side by side. They did not match; they did not nearly match. Where the hell did that leave them? Weston was in no way associated with the hack. There had been a mix up. All those days of interviews and careful collection of DNA samples had been a complete waste of time. They could not possibly run the interviews again – even if they had the time, people would be suspicious. If it got out that they were looking for illegally obtained DNA samples, there would be hell to pay. The Met. would get to hear what was going on and she would be out of a job.

'Ah hell,' she muttered as she turned the evidence bag over and stared once again at that damned number 87932.

Hang on a minute. A lump formed in her throat. She picked up a specimen lens and held it to her eye. Focussing on the number 3 of the five digits, it slowly dawned on her that the white opaque square on which the number had been written was flawed. Somewhere in the manufacturing process the underlying smooth plastic had failed to take up the high friction coating and left a tiny slick blemish over which Sharkey's pen had slipped without leaving a down stroke. This was not a 3; it was either an 8 or a 9. The index number was 87982 or 87992, not 87932. She calmed herself. One of those two people was her perp., she was sure of it. Her nose for the minutia of detective work, and for coffee, had not let her down.

She picked up the suspect folders that related to the two numbers: Francis Bordelay and Seth Whitten.

'Which one of you is it?'

Franks leafed through the two documents, reading the profiles. It was a slam dunk. Bordelay was a 45-year-old lab technician with a drink problem and a gammy knee. Whitten was a computer whizz-with a Cambridge degree.

'Well, Mr Whitten, let's see who your friends are.'

With a look of triumph she picked up the phone.

'George, put a tail on Whitten. Stay close to him. If he takes a piss I want to know it's your shoes he's splashing.'

CHAPTER 4

While he was good with computers, Seth was no counter-espionage agent. He knew how to protect his identity when it came to hacking but he did not have a breeze when it came to the physical world. Naïve didn't go there. The heroes on the telly always knew when they were being followed, the shady guy with the turned up coat collar quickly looking into the shop window when the pursued looked back. How difficult could it be to spot a tail?

Seth had never heard of 'the box', the four-person team that surrounded a quarry. If he crossed the road there was still someone in front and behind. If he turned up an alley, 1 redirected 2, 3 and 4 to pick him up again at the other end. If he jumped in a taxi, they tracked his phone. His every move was followed and reported: who he spoke to, what he bought, where he ate. His phone conversations were tapped. Casual conversations with his friends were picked up on directional microphones. To all this, Seth was totally oblivious.

Franks had decided to let him run for a few days to see if she could pull anyone else into the net, see who else he had involved. Her instructions were to identify the hacker or hackers and then detain them, after which she would receive further instructions. Sharkey had been informed of Seth's involvement and had agreed to the extension of the surveillance to identify any other conspirators. He, in turn, had informed Yat-sen, who had dispatched a specialist team from Shanghai. It would be there in less than 24 hours.

It was Seth's bike that had proved to be Franks' Achilles' heel. Only 12 hours previously, surveillance had been put in place. Connie had stayed the night but had exams the following day. They both left early. Connie walked back to her flat for a few hours of emergency cramming and Seth cycled off to the gym. He decided to leave his phone behind, as Connie would not be calling him and he did not want it falling out of his bike shorts – again.

Within minutes of their departure, the technical squad moved in and thoroughly bugged the flat. A team of two pursuit cars, one in front, one behind, tracked him to the gym. There was a small level of anxiety when it became apparent that he was not carrying his phone but his light attire and direction of travel soon made his ultimate destination clear. The 'box' was waiting for him when he arrived and monitored his calisthenics for the hour he sweated it out.

Seth decided to do a loop of the park on the way back to Fernley House. The cycle lane crossed a set of pedestrian lights, which turned red as he approached. He vaguely noticed a car slowing up as he neared the crossing. *Hmm – LN- London plates*, he thought as he narrowly avoided colliding with a mother pushing a pram onto the crossing. She shouted some abuse as he sped through and he looked back to get a better view of his latest near miss when, to his horror, the car he had just passed also failed to stop and knocked over the buggy. Slamming on its breaks, it was rear ended by another car. The mother was screaming and the child, still strapped into the buggy, was now jammed under the front bumper of the lead car, which had been pushed over the crossing by the rear impact.

But the driver and the passenger of the car were not looking at the carnage they had just created – they were looking at him. For a split second all they were interested in was the guy on the bike already 30m away. Their look told him everything.

As Seth's predicament dawned, raw instinct took over. He was off the road and barrelling down a footpath into the park before he even knew what he was doing. The path wound between the trees like an alpine slalom. He chanced a quick backward glance almost piling into the trunk of a huge Sequoya. He caught it a glancing blow, the handlebars digging into the soft bark, nearly ripping them from his grasp. As he recovered his balance, he narrowly avoided ploughing down an old couple out for a stroll in the sunshine. He slowed his pace, confident that he had put enough distance between himself and his pursuers, who must now be on foot.

Oh God, what had he done! They were tracking him, whoever they were. He couldn't go back to the flat; they would almost certainly be waiting for him there. If he carried on across the park he was sure he would be picked up on the other side. He needed to hide, and quickly.

Jumping off his bike, he lifted it up and put it on his shoulder. Turning into the densest part of the woods, he ran a zigzag route away from the path until he found what he was looking for. Ahead was a large horse chestnut tree in full leaf. There were several low-lying branches and the upper canopy was dense to the point of solidity.

Seth laid the bike down carefully so as not to disturb the leaf litter. He removed a pen knife and spare inner tube from the small zipper pouch under the bike's seat. He quickly cut through the tube, tying one end to the front wheel. Throwing the other end over a low branch, he hauled the bike up into the tree. Once on the first branch, he removed the front and rear wheels, carrying them higher up the trunk and wedging them out of sight. The frame, now more manageable, he strapped to his back with the inner tube and climbed as high as he could, repeatedly snagging branches with protruding bits of pedal and forks, leaving him exhausted.

Looking down from his perch, he could not see the ground. If he could not see the ground, then no one on the ground could see him. Unless his pursuers were going to climb every tree in the park, or they had Tonto to spot the bent blades of grass and the snapped twig, they were not going to find him up here.

Seth squatted down with his back against the trunk and settled in for a long wait. He would not come down 'til night fell. Hopefully by then they would have given up and assumed he had slipped through their clutches. Almost at once he heard voices coming through the woods. He would be amazed if it was a search team already but that is exactly what it was. How the hell had they got here so fast and in such numbers? From the muffled voices below he guessed there were just two of them. Either they were expert trackers or, as he suspected, merely part of a sweep moving through the park. The swiftly fading voices confirmed the latter and he could breathe again.

* * * * *

Seth woke with a start. There was a crippling pain in his knees from the hunched position he had assumed in the branches. He could just make out the reflection of the neon street lights on the cloud cover through the few branches left above his head. He listened intently. All he heard was the sound of blood rushing in his ears and the faraway whine of a low-powered motorcycle. It must be late. He looked at his watch, a light touch and the Tissot's red illumination showed him that it was 10 pm. He retrieved the wheels from their arboreal hiding places and again, with the frame strapped to his back, shinnied down the tree.

When he had reassembled it on the ground,

he walked the bike cautiously through the under-growth. If they had left anyone behind, they would probably be at one of the pedestrian exits to the park so he climbed over the perimeter fence at the pointy east end where the road bent away to the left and right, giving no clear view of his departure from either side. Across the road was a small lane-way. He waited for a late night bus to round the bend and sped across as it passed; ensuring that at least one side of his escape was masked. Once down the lane, he crouched behind a garden gate, peering out to see if he had been followed. The road was clear. He headed for the lock-up outside town and for Hillary.

Although an avowed environmentalist, Seth had one weakness and that was his passion for Hillary. This rivalled even his feelings for Connie, as Hillary was his first love. He was so ashamed of this that no one at the college knew about Hillary, who was kept in a lock-up 9 miles out of town. Her registration plate HYL 4Y was the origin of the name. She was his pride and joy.

He had seen her on *Auto Trader*. The owners clearly had no idea of her value. Because she was a left-hand drive they probably thought few people would be interested in her. But the 1990 Lancia Delta HF Integrale was never made in a right-hand drive version and Seth paid the asking price of £1,500 with no questions asked. This was a classic car of impeccable pedigree. Although, on the surface an ordinary-looking small family car, the HF Integrale variant was a four-wheel-drive, supercharged hot hatch rally car with a carbon footprint the size of Belgium.

It was in this lock-up that Seth kept all his most valuable toys: a Samsung tablet computer and an Iridium satellite phone. The tablet was a doozy (as the Yanks would say). It was not just the fact that it was so light, thin and powerful that made it his calculating machine of choice. With no keyboard, no hard drive (128 GB of flash ram!) and the latest LED backlit touch screen, it was unbelievably parsimonious with its use of power.

The sat. phone was one of the more bizarre 21st birthday gifts he had received from his Great Uncle Harry. Harry Cumbor was a lifelong traveller. He had never married and had spent most of his time roaming the world on some great expedition or other. Seth had received many birthday calls from his uncle on a similar phone from outlandish locales such as the Hindu Kush or the South Col of Everest.

Seth lay on the cramped back seat of the Lancia. The black leather stuck to his sweaty skin like Sellotape. His thighs burned as if someone had poured boiling water over them. The exertions of the 9 mile dash had been temporarily incapacitating and he needed to recoup his energy before he could think about what to do next. He was certain this hideout was secure – at least for the moment. The monthly rent of £50 was paid, in cash, to the resident of the council house to which the garage was attached. He rarely saw his landlord. Most months he just pushed the money through the letter box. There was no paperwork.

If Connie had known about this place he would have been concerned. Not that he thought that Connie would betray him; just that she might let the information slip or volunteer Hillary's location. She could have no idea of the predicament he was in and there was no safe way to tell her he was all right. By now she would be frantic. There had never been a day since they had got together that they had not been in constant contact. She must know something was wrong. He had not called her. She always imagined the worst and in this case she could be right.

His very survival depended on his ability to remain off the radar. That meant no phone calls, no credit card use and no visits to familiar places. While the garage was a safe haven, he could really only stay here tonight. His landlord was bound to spot him and at the very least object to him setting up home in his lock-up. More likely he would terminate the arrangement and find another tenant. No security of tenure here. He had cashed his monthly grant cheque and still had £400 in his wallet. This would feed him for a few weeks but would not put a roof over his head for more than a couple of nights. Panic began to well up in his chest. He suddenly felt very alone and frightened.

Thinking about his pursuers, Seth realised that they were not the police. There was no way that they would have or could have raised those sorts of resources to track him down and have him followed in such a short time. It had been only three days since he had been interviewed by Sharkey. If they had known he was the hacker, they would have picked him up at the time. No, they were fishing and something he had said must have given him away. But he hadn't said anything, just denied any involvement, drunk his coffee and left. There was nothing that could possibly link him to the leaked information. He kept all the hacked data in the Cloud. Even Connie did not know where it was. They could look at his desktop computer all they liked, they would find nothing. No data, no links, no nothing. Whenever he accessed the web, he used InPrivate Browsing, leaving no trace of his transactions.

At least he had the tablet; it was totally portable and would give him access to the web. He could sit in a cyber café and use their Wi-Fi. This was totally anonymous but he was afraid they might be watching such establishments, so there were risks involved. But hey, there was Uncle Harry's sat. phone! Satellite communications were so expensive for normal mortals that he had never bothered to test the service – he had had no need up 'til now. With a little ingenuity he would be able to penetrate the defences of his pay-as-you-go account with Motorola and get it to give him free access to the Iridium network and call Connie. She must be so worried.

But power was going to be a problem. He could use the car. It had a 12 volt converter that he sometimes used to power his mobile phone when he was on long journeys, but taking the car anywhere risked detection. He was the registered owner. If his pursuers had any cop-on they would already have been on to Swansea vehicle licensing centre and pulled his details. He could put on false plates but a red Integrale with false plates would stick out like a sore thumb. The car was out.

He lay back and his eyes roamed over the beautiful black leather Recaro interior. He loved this car. His eyes rested on the 12 volt plug in the lighter socket. He traced the wire that ran up and through the chink in the top of the passenger window and out through the garage door – that was it, the solar cell trickle charger. He had his power source for his tablet and his sat. phone. Why hadn't he thought of it before – and him a researcher in renewable energy?

The wire he was looking at was attached to a solar panel resting on the roof of the garage. He had been prompted to buy the unit shortly after he purchased the Lancia. The car's battery had not been in the best of condition and, after only a few days of not being used, the charge leaked away to such an extent that the motor would not start. The main culprit was the anti-theft alarm. While it only used a small amount of charge, it was enough to kill the old battery. A trip to the local motor factor had introduced him to the high cost of replacement batteries but also to the wonders of the solar panel trickle charger. Ever one for the latest gadget, Seth had snapped up a unit and Hillary had been kept in juice ever since. All he had to do was charge the sat. phone and he could call Connie.

* * * * *

'Mobile one to control – we've been made.'

'Jesus, is he still in sight?'

'Negative. Returning to the apartment – hoping to re-acquire there. Request backup to attend girlfriend's apartment.'

'You better hope you do.'

Franks was mad. She had him! She had him and she let him get away. He was a resourceful little bastard, she would give him that. To manage to evade, never mind spot, her pursuit team was a feat in itself.

'George, any movement at the girlfriend's flat?'

'No, Ma'am, she is still at the university. There have been no calls to her mobile, but she has reported Whitten to the police as a missing person. Unless she is bluffing and using a pay phone or a mobile we are not aware of, she has not been in touch with Whitten and is genuinely unaware of his location.'

'Do you have eyes on her?'

'Yes, Ma'am.'

'For God's sake don't lose her as well. She is our only point of contact.'

Franks' mobile rang. It was the Met. Her blood froze. She had told HQ about a holiday in Norwich, catching up with old friends, a reasonable cover for her clandestine off-the-grid work. What in the world were they doing trying to contact her on holiday? Had someone grassed her up? She took the call.

'Commander, what can I do for you?'

'Inspector, sorry to bother you on your vacation but we have been asked to assist in a missing person's case. Norwich is a bit stretched, what with cutbacks and the like, and has requested bodies to conduct interviews. Was wondering if you wouldn't mind putting in a few hours? Show willing, interdepartmental cooperation and all that. Go down well at budget time.'

'Would be delighted. I was getting a bit bored to be honest. Seeing old friends again that you have lost touch with reminds you why you lost touch with them in the first place.'

'Ha-ha, yes, too true. Time off in lieu of course.'

'Much obliged. Will get straight on to it.'

She replaced the receiver. *There is a God!* This opened up a whole new level of resource. She could now openly go after Whitten. She would have the entire Norwich beat as eyes on the ground to support her and he would have – nobody.

PART II

It is difficult to get a man to understand something, when his salary depends on his not understanding it.

Upton Sinclair

Mai Lee wiped away the tears with the back of her dirt-encrusted hand. Yoon Chong's limp body lay flat against the slatted boards of the box-frame bed that had been his prison for the past three months. It seemed like only yesterday that their only son, a product of the strict one-child policy of the Chinese elite, had been a strapping 15-year-old, labouring on the smallholding that had lifted his family out of what otherwise would have been a miserable existence. Daily he toiled under the yoke of the local crime boss, Temüjin, whose rule held sway over the nearby rare earth refinery. Yoon Chong was to have been his parents' guarantee against the penury of old age.

His sister, their firstborn, had been spared the destitution that was visited upon so many girls who had the misfortune to be raised in this private piece of hell that was the city of Bayan-Ovoo. She had died at birth, like so many other Chinese babies cursed with the double X chromosome. After a difficult delivery, her husband had told Mai Lee that Sing Ying had been stillborn. But she had heard her cry, that pitiful mewling cry of a new-born that had torn at her heart like a tiger's claw. And now her son would be taken, leaving her alone to endure the last few miserable years that the foul dust belching from People's Factory number 8 would allow.

The local health inspector had blamed the poor rice harvest. He said the boy should get better in a few weeks with good food and careful nursing. He could not meet Mai Lee's eyes; they both knew it was a lie. There was no money for the medicines to treat Yoon Chong. Not that there was anything on this earth that could help him now. Leukaemia had wasted his once strong body, as it had his cousin and several other members of the extended Yee family. It was *like a plague across the countryside. The health inspector walked quickly away down the dusty path to his brand new Mitsubishi Shogun. Once inside, the medic changed his face mask, throwing the used one onto the road and switched the air con to recycle. There was nothing the inspector could do for these people; that did not mean that his own son should not benefit from Temüjin's largesse.*

Yoon Chong breathed his last. His mother had no more tears to give. It was as much with relief as sorrow that she placed her hand over her son's staring eyes and closed his lids for the last time. His suffering was finally over; she felt envious of him, even a little angry that he had left her behind. They had both paid a very heavy price for the West's love affair with green energy.

CHAPTER 5

From his vantage point high on the valley ridge, Randolph van Klaveren gazed out of his lounge window over the village rooftops and across the islands to where the 'dark Mourne' swept down to the sea. He slumped back into his leather armchair as he regained his breath from the excesses of his early morning torture regime. The 5K daily run round the hill maintained his toned physique. He may be retired but that did not mean he was going to let himself go to seed.

He stabbed the TV remote to be assailed by an argument playing out on Sky News. Someone the press had dubbed 'Deep Cool', no doubt in a nod to ex US President Nixon's Watergate affair and the infamous 'Deep Throat', had blown the whistle on the goings-on at the keepers of the world's temperature in England and the pros and antis were going at it hammer and tongs...

The harsh ring tone of his mobile snapped him back to reality.

'Uncle Randy?'

'Connie, how are you?'

The call came from his god-daughter Constance, the only child of a long-deceased friend from college days in England.

'To what do I owe this most pleasant interlude in my boring old day?'

The unexpected response bubbled out of the phone like a torrent.

'Thank God I caught you. I don't know where to start...You know I'm doing my masters in Renewable Energy at Norwich Uni... Well, I met this boy...'

'Congratulations! Do I hear wedding bells?'

'No, nothing like that. That's not why I'm ringing.'

He could feel the level of frustration building in her voice. Perhaps he was pushing the jolly uncle thing a bit too much; he decided to back off.

'Sorry, didn't mean to embarrass you. I was only teasing. Go on – you were saying?'

'Well, Seth, that's his name – he's in the same year as me – Oh Uncle Randy he's gone missing.'

The panic in her voice was palpable. Randolph now deeply regretted the flippant remark he had made about marriage, but then, how was he to know?

'Ah pet, that's awful. Have you contacted the police?'

Randolph was floundering. The girl was obviously seriously stressed but it was not clear why she was ringing him. What could he do? Why didn't she contact her mother? Surely she was the one who should be handling this sort of domestic emergency?

'Yes, yes! I've contacted the police.'

'So have they given you any idea as to how they are progressing with their search for him?'

'You don't understand, Uncle Randy; they say they are treating him as a missing person but they've taken away all his computer gear. I think they believe he's "Deep Cool", who leaked the "Climategate" e-mails.'

'Yes – just heard about that on the news. Something about scientists using a trick to make global warming look worse? The police think Seth is Deep Cool?' Randolph was having difficulty getting his head around the implications of what Connie was telling him.

'So what you're saying is that the police think your boyfriend is the whistle-blower who has leaked e-mails from Norwich University's climate centre. Well, has he?' Randolph was aghast.

'I'm not sure – probably. I think there is a lot more going on than we know, I need you, Uncle Randy – I don't trust the police.'

* * * * *

The newspaper article gave Randolph a sinking feeling. Deep Cool had breached security at Norwich University and leaked some juicy morsels onto the Internet and the police were in hot pursuit. The media hacks had been working overtime to sensationalise what, to most, would be something of a dry subject – global warming – by hanging a flash moniker on the fugitive. Now here he was arriving at Norwich University in search of a missing computer whizz-kid. Could Constance be wrong about her boyfriend? He dearly hoped so.

Connie was waiting for him on the platform at Norwich train station. Randolph could tell she was upset but managing to hold it together. The makeup was immaculate as always but it could not disguise the level of distress showing in her face. He kissed her tenderly on the cheek; she hugged him but did not speak.

'Come on, I'm gasping for a drink. There's a great pub on the river near here. I remember it from my football supporter days – the Complete Angler. Do you know it?'

She nodded and with some pretence at normality, accompanied him out of the station and across the river bridge. The bar was empty at that time of day, not as he remembered it from his time as a follower of Derby County.

'So tell me how you got into all of this, and why you think Seth is this so-called "Deep Cool".'

Connie filled him in on Seth's hacking of Sharkey's e-mails and the promise he had made to her not to do anything dangerous.

'Well, then it probably wasn't him,' opined Randolph.

She gave him one of those contemptuous stares that so reminded him of his ex-wife.

'I know it was him. He had access to all the data. Sharkey would have known at once it was him. We discussed it and that is why I got him to *promise* not to do anything dangerous before I would help him.'

'What do you mean? You helped him?'

Randolph was starting to get nervous. They were about to meet up with CID at Wymondham, the HQ of the Norfolk Constabulary. His initial thoughts were that this would be a fairly relaxed affair. Connie would tell the detective that she knew Seth and was concerned for his whereabouts. They would take down the details as she knew them: when she had seen him last, where he might go, did he have any enemies, that sort of thing, and then get to it and find him. This now seemed a rather forlorn hope. Clearly Seth did not want to be found. All the more concerning to Randy, he had wantonly involved his precious god-daughter in a conspiracy that could, at the very least, end her academic career and, worst-case scenario, might actually land her in gaol. What the hell was this guy playing at? Let him ruin his own life if he wanted to but leave others out of it.

'What is it exactly that you helped him to do?'

'Well, to begin with, it was just a matter of reading the decrypted e-mails between Professor Sharkey and Professor Yat-sen.'

'YOU WHAT? You were reading private e-mails between two university professors that Seth had decrypted?'

'Keep your voice down! We don't want the whole pub to know what I've done,' Connie hissed.

'And who is this Yat-sen character anyway?' The typically Western xenophobia, lying just beneath the surface, showed its face with Randolph's rising stress levels. 'I don't like the sound of him.'

'He was once accused of misappropriating grant aid from the US government but now he's President Mecheri's science Tsar. He and Sharkey had something to do with carbon trading, which had got them very excited.'

'All very interesting Connie but is any of this going to be of use when we meet with the police?'

This was going nowhere. They needed to plan something she could say tomorrow that was not going to be incriminating or suspicious or both and this line of conversation was not helping.

'Look, did you actually help Seth get any of this material?'

'No.'

'Good. Then all you did was help him with a bit of research to do with climate change, right?'

Plausible deniability, that's what they needed. How could she know the source of the e-mails or what Seth was up to? After all, she was just a dumb blonde.

Connie was great at doing the dumb blonde, that and the fact that she had a brain as big as a planet was an irresistible combination to some men who had managed to escape the Neanderthal swamp. Yes, that is how they would play it, Randolph thought. What could Connie possibly have known about Seth's plans? All she was interested in was makeup and glossy magazines (note to self, buy a copy of *Hello!* magazine on the way to the Cop Shop). In fact, what had she been doing when she realised that he was missing? Going back to pick up her makeup bag! Randolph outlined the rather flimsy plan and Connie jumped at it. She had spent her short adult life being underestimated; now she could put that experience to good use. Perhaps this could work.

* * * * *

'Thank you for coming, Constance, I know this must be very upsetting for you.'

Inspector Franks came across as a mild-mannered, southern-accented woman in her late thirties. Possibly privately educated – definitely a fast track candidate, destined for high office, odd that she should be posted to such a backwater as Norwich, thought Randolph.

'Now let me tell you how the process works. You are not under arrest; you are not under caution so anything you say to me cannot be used against you in the future. All we are interested in is finding Mr Whitten as quickly as possible.'

'Likewise,' Randolph chipped in.

Franks shot him a cold glance but then immediately softened. 'And of course, Mr van Klaveren, thank you for coming such a long way to be with Constance at this difficult time.'

Too late, lady. He had taken an immediate dislike to the woman – Connie needed to be careful dealing with her. She was not the sugar and spice and all things nice she was trying to be.

'You sound as though you are a long way

from home yourself, Inspector,' Randolph responded.

'Quite so. Well spotted. Yes, I am on secondment from the Met. Now, Connie – may I call you Connie? – will you please take me through the last two weeks preceding Seth's disappearance?'

Who was this woman? Randolph thought. She was far too eager to deflect attention from what she was doing here. This was no ordinary missing person's interview. Connie had been right to bring backup. They had assumed that the interview would be conducted by a man. He had to admit sexism was alive and well and living in his subconscious however much he would like to think that it was not. Connie's feminine wiles were unlikely to work on this occasion.

'As I'm sure you know, Seth and I are an item.'

'Sorry?'

'We are going out together, boyfriend, girlfriend, you know.'

'Yes, sorry. I was not familiar with the term. Please, continue.'

'Seth and I are both postgrads. As for the last few weeks, well, I'm not sure that they have been any different from any other time.'

Good girl, just play dumb, thought Randolph.

'Naturally, we were looking forward to the summer hols; we planned to go to Spain for a couple of weeks. They are one of Europe's leaders in the field of wind energy generation—'

Franks cut in.

'Thanks for that, but could I just bring you back to the time preceding Seth's disappearance? Had you noticed any change in his behaviour? Was he depressed or anxious about anything?'

'No, not that I noticed, and that is what is so worrying. We are really close. He tells me everything. We do everything together. The guys on the course call us Romeo and Juliet. I just don't know what's happened to him.'

The tears welled up in Connie's eyes. Randolph couldn't tell if they were real or she was just faking it.

'Can I get you a glass of water?'

'Yes, please,' Connie murmured.

The Inspector left the room, returning a few minutes later with a glass of chilled water and a box of tissues. Connie plucked one, dabbed her eyes and gave her nose a good blow.

'I'm sorry about that. I want to help in any way I can. I just want him back safe.'

A faint look of exasperation flickered across Franks' face while she tried again.

'So, I know this is an anxious time for you but is there anything you can think of that might give us a clue as to why Seth might have disappeared?'

'No. I've told you, I just want him back.' Connie broke down, sobbing.

At this point Randolph cut in.

'Look, I don't think this is helping, Inspector. Clearly there is nothing she can tell you that is going to be of use. I'm staying at Seth's flat in Fernley House for as long as it takes. If you have anything for us, please contact me there.'

Franks reluctantly gave up.

'We'll keep you informed of any progress.'

They bade her farewell and left the building. A heavyset man entered the interview room. Franks did not look up.

'She's hiding something. Follow them. I want 24-hour surveillance'

'Yes, Gov.'

'And find out more on this van Klaveren character. Who the hell appointed him as her minder?'

He closed the door behind him as he left. From the direction of Franks' mobile, strains of the theme tune to 'Hawaii Five-O' filled the room. She took the call.

'Yes? They've gone. No – she's hiding something. She doesn't know where he is but she's not telling all she knows. I've put a tail on them and they're bugged. If he contacts her, we'll have him.'

CHAPTER 6

Connie drove Randolph back to Seth's flat. It was a mess. Whoever had searched it had done a thorough job. They set-to, putting everything back in its place. The police were not treating it as a crime scene, which on one level relieved Connie but on the other hand she was surprised that they had not fingerprinted the place. They had not catalogued missing items. Wasn't that standard police work? She shared her thoughts with Randolph.

'I agree. Things are not adding up. This Franks woman is way too senior to be involved in a simple missing person's case and while I am not minimising your acting ability, I don't think she believed a word you said and yet she had no reason not to. Like us, I think she knows more than she is letting on.'

'What do you mean acting? Seth has been missing for two days now. He hasn't rung me. If he was OK he would have tried to contact me. I am terrified something has happened to him. What are we going to do, Randy?'

Randolph put a fatherly arm around her shoulders and hugged her to him. She was right:

the situation was looking grave. For Seth to have left without a note, or make any attempt to contact Connie, made him fear the worst but he was not about to admit that to her. He wanted to keep her spirits up. It was going to be tough enough dealing with the police as it was. He needed her support and ideas if they were going to find Seth. She was smart and he needed those smarts firing on all cylinders, not wallowing in a pool of self-pity.

'Come on, Connie. What else did Seth tell you he found out? He's clearly no fool.'

'There were a lot of e-mails between Yat-sen, the Stanford lecturer, and Seth's head of college, Professor Sharkey. Seth thought that the college was getting illegal funding from China for promoting the global warming agenda and Yat-sen might be involved somehow.'

'If he is right about that, Seth might have worried about being targeted by these people and that they would try to get to him through you. He would be crazy to try to get in contact.'

'What do you mean? Do you think we are being followed?'

It hadn't occurred to him, but if that was the case, then Seth would have realised that big money was at stake here.

* * * * *

The bugs carried out their task with silent efficiency, relaying the conversation in all its high tech clarity.

'They are suspicious of you, Ma'am. They do not know where Whitten is and have not been contacted by him. They clearly are not surveillance aware but think that it may be a possibility.'

'Stay on them. Do we have any information yet on van Klaveren?'

'Yes, Ma'am – military training. He is ex-Irish Rangers, now retired. Has contacts in both Ireland and the UK. Active during the Troubles, close protection work – not to be underestimated.'

Damn, that's all they needed, some wannabe Irish Rambo, Franks thought. She could do without his kind. Well, he was not being very smart at the moment. He certainly had not considered the possibility of Whitten's flat being bugged. He was out of the frame for any involvement in the hack, but the girlfriend was a different matter. Clearly she knew what Whitten was up to. Her level of involvement, however, seemed superficial. Her level of attachment was very high. Maybe that could be useful should they fail to re-acquire.

Time was slipping by. Sharkey was getting impatient. A preliminary examination of Whitten's hard drive had revealed little more than lecture notes and thesis work, but more importantly she had not as yet located the data. It was this more than anything else that Sharkey was looking for. The hacker had been identified; he was pleased about that. That the hacker was still on the loose did not please him at all; that the hacked data was still out there was his deepest concern.

And he wasn't the only one.

＊ ＊ ＊ ＊ ＊

Professor Jiang Yat-sen had been summoned to Shanghai. The Sum Yop Tong were his paymasters; they owned him and when they called, one did not question their reasons – one simply obeyed.

Yat-sen was effectively an indentured slave. His family's escape from the terror of Mao's Cultural Revolution had begun on the Wampu River, on a junk supplied by the Snake Heads to get them to the sea and then on a perilous journey down the coast to Hong Kong, where his heavily pregnant mother stowed aboard a freighter bound for Hawaii. He was born on that boat, somewhere between Midway Island and Oahu. His mother never made it to Honolulu. Her body unceremoniously tossed overboard, it was now baby Jiang's job to pay for the journey.

The Snake Heads were patient people. They had to be; it took years, sometimes generations, for their cargo to pay back the cost of their passage to these notorious 'people traffickers'. They had begun their trade in the 1800s, supplying Chinese coolies to work on the US transcontinental railway.

As America's need for cheap labour declined, the Snake Heads morphed into people smugglers. In the West, they were seen as the worst sort of barbarians, leeching off the misery of displaced peoples. In the East they were heroes, latter-day

Scarlet Pimpernels spiriting the poor and dispossessed from the starvation and torment of pre-communist Imperial China to the bright lights and freedom of the land of opportunity.

Yat-sen was raised in the Chinatown area of San Francisco. One of his earliest memories was of his foster mother explaining to him how he must work hard at school so that he would one day be able to pay his debt to the Snake Heads, who effectively held his mother's family hostage back in Shanghai.

And Yat-sen did work hard. He won a scholarship to MIT, then to Stanford. He was a full Professor with tenure at the astonishingly young age of 27. But he would never pay off the Snake Heads. When it became apparent what a prodigy they had, they sold his debt to the Sum Yop Tong. This, to all intents and purposes, made him a gang member, whether he wanted to be or not, and the only way anyone left the Tong was in a pine box.

The 13-hour, transpolar flight from New York passed surprisingly quickly. A significant perk of senior academic status at Stanford was first-class travel. The bed was comfortable, the champagne vintage and the cabin staff attentive. It was not often that the Tong would call him. He did not relish frequent contact with the criminal organisation to which he was allied. No one but a few senior members of the Tong itself even knew of his links and he wanted to keep it that way.

The 430kph journey from Shanghai airport to the city centre on the Transrapid Train never failed to impress. The Matrix-like antigravity manoeuvre as the train maintained its speed on the long left-hand curve always spooked him and the sudden thunderclap as the Transrapid met its sister train coming the other way at a closing speed of almost 900kph made him jump every time. His destination was floor 101, of the half kilometre high World Financial Centre or, as it had quickly become known, the 'Bottle Opener Building' due to the large square void near the top designed to prevent the skyscraper from being blown over in high winds.

'Professor Yat-sen, you honour us with your presence.'

Chew Tin Gop addressed Yat-sen with apparent deference and self-deprecation, a hangover from the time of the mogul emperors, who would fête the leadership of a conquered nation, serving great feasts from gold and silver tableware while the Emperor would eat from crude wooden plates and drink from rough pottery beakers. The message was clear: 'I am so superior to you in every way that I need no trappings of wealth or overt demonstrations of power to show how far beneath me you lie.' Such was the greeting from the head of China's largest Tong, the Chinese equivalent of the Mafia's *Capo di Capo*, the boss of bosses.

'You have grave news you wish to impart, but you are a clever man, Professor, and you also have a remedy for the predicament in which we find ourselves – is that not so?'

'Yes, *ah kung*.' Yat-sen addressed Chew with

the familiar 'Grandfather' implying a close relationship that, in fact, was far from warm. 'An Englishman has unknowingly uncovered links between our contacts in the West and our business interests in Ömnögovi province.'

'How can this be? Is this man a member of the British Secret Service of whom we were not aware – has this master of espionage penetrated to the very core of our society without our knowledge?'

The question was like a sliver of ice through Yat-sen's heart. Chew had been fully informed of Yat-sen's failure to protect his links to Sharkey, but to attempt to hide this would ensure a swift and ruthless response. His only hope was to offer a solution to the problem that was plausible and acceptable to the Tong Master.

'His name is Whitten and he attends Norwich University, in England, a student of our associate, Professor Sharkey. It is through him that our plan has been revealed.'

'Has Sharkey betrayed us? He must pay with his life!'

Chew was playing with Yat-sen and he knew it.

'No, Master. It is Whitten who is the betrayer; he has stolen information from Sharkey that may lead him to divine our intent. We will apprehend him and retrieve the information. If he were to reveal what he knows…' Yat-sen's voice trailed off.

'And where is this man – his capture is imminent, is that not so?'

'Yes, yes, we are tracking him in Norwich – a small town in eastern England. He cannot escape. It is but a matter of a few days.'

'Recover the information, dispose of the Englishman, let Sharkey know of his fate, let him be assured this will be his fate also should our plans be endangered again. You may leave.'

Yat-sen bowed and backed out of the room. He had survived, but for how much longer? Whitten had proved impossible for Franks to find. The man was like a wraith. At any moment he could publicise the illegal funding to the university and Yat-sen's relationship with the US President would be at an end. He would have to bring in a professional. Yat-sen made the call.

CHAPTER 7

Seth had gone native; they would never find him. The fens of East Anglia had been the refuge of many a tortured soul over the centuries, from Celtic tribes evading the Roman conquest to Catholic priests dodging Cromwell's armies during the Reformation to latter-day convicts on the run from Norwich Gaol. Seth preferred to lump himself in with the Celtic tribes. They had been masters of the fen, with secret trails and hidden encampments on the numerous raised mounds that dotted this reed sea.

Strumpshaw fen was particularly convenient for the Environmental Studies students from Norwich University. Just three stops down the line from Norwich train station, the eco warriors, as the locals from the nearby Buckenham estate fondly referred to them, would pile out of the carriages and fan out into the marshy ground just a few feet from Station Road. This had been Seth's hunting ground for the last two years. He knew the area like the back of his hand and had often camped out for days, monitoring water quality and wind speeds.

The fens were ideal locations for large wind farms as they were on a flat uninterrupted plane, exposed to the prevailing east wind off the North Sea. One summer Seth had spent an entire week mapping the mounds as they led away from the station and devising convoluted routes through them like a Victorian garden maze; only in this situation, if you got lost, you died of exposure or drowned in the bog.

This idle waste of summer time was now going to provide him with a mobile hideout. There were 37 mounds suitable for habitation within 5 miles of the station, so he could move every night. There was a risk in staying so close to Buckenham but he needed to get food.

His first priority when he arrived was to make a camouflaged shelter before darkness fell. He extracted his mound map and made his way through the reeds for 2 miles southeast into the deepest part of the swamp, as far away from the river and dry land as he could get. Here he set up camp on hill 16. Of course 'hill' was something of a misnomer really; they were just areas of ground not much more than a few inches above the water table. The 37 mounds had built up over the decades. They were constantly shifting; no more than random accumulations of silt topped with reed matting providing refuge and nesting sites for herons and other wading birds as well as recalcitrant students evading the long arm of the law.

Hill 16 did not protrude above the surrounding reed beds. If it had, it would have been rather useless for the purpose he had in mind. No, the reeds appeared as a featureless swathe of light green sandwiched between the brown muddy snake of the River Yare and the railway line to Great Yarmouth. Nobody would spot him.

* * * * *

Seth's night in the reeds had been a relatively comfortable affair. The bivouac had stayed completely dry and if anything, he had been too warm. Today he would experiment with the technology. The previous day had been sunny and had enabled him to set the sat. phone and the tablet charging while he waded through the swamp to break up any scent trails he might have left. The uplink was easy-peasy. Just like sitting at his desk in Fernley House, except that he was laid flat out on a bed of reeds just 3 inches above the dark waters of the Norfolk fens.

Now he could begin to think again about what had got him into this mess in the first place. He took out his sat. phone and tablet, which were secured from the elements in waterproof transparent Ziploc bags, so no matter how filthy and wet Seth got, they would stay snug and dry. He began to run searches on the e-mail data. He was looking for links between Yat-sen, Sharkey and other academics within the tens of thousands of e-mails he had copied.

He could not possibly read every mail before his money would run out. The only sensible way of searching the e-mail data was to let the computer do the hard work; sifting through irrelevant stuff, winnowing the wheat from the chaff. Fortunately, he could run these algorithms in the Cloud, checking in on them from time to time to monitor their progress. The next step was to run similar search algorithms but on the internet itself. What he was hoping to find was some correlation between individuals who had corresponded with Norwich University and activities they were involved with outside academia. After setting the programs in motion he went back to see what had shown up in the e-mails.

As Seth delved deeper into the correspondence between Sharkey and Yat-sen, he knew that he had bitten off more than he could chew. It had not taken him long to establish why the Sharkey-Yat-sen e-mails were encrypted and the others were not: it was at Yat-sen's insistence.

Yat-sen had begun to channel significant funds into Norwich University's Climate Centre, but Seth had never heard about this – and he didn't think any of his colleagues had either. Millions of dollars, ostensibly coming from the People's Republic of China Ministry of Education 'to further research into the damaging impact of carbon pollution on the environment with particular focus on mitigation and the development of non-carbon renewable energy sources…' This did not ring true.

Seth had been to China. He had stood in the Olympic Village in Beijing. In the noon-day sun in May he could not see from the Bird's Nest stadium to the large blue soap dish that was the Olympic pool – a distance of less than a mile. The pollution had to be seen to be believed. The yellow disk of the sun was never visible even out as far as the Great Wall – the pall was there too. On a trip to see the tombs of the Ming Emperors he had observed the grotesque sight of migrant Chinese workers tying plastic bags over individual fruit on trees to protect them from the toxic air and rain. It was clear that China didn't give a flying fuck about the environment.

But this was not just about China trying to put on a clean face and parade its environmental credentials to the world. There was more to it than that. Why the secrecy? Why the need to 'hide the decline'? He still believed that Sharkey was an idealist, albeit an idealist who thought that the end justified the means, but for Yat-sen it was something entirely different.

He lay back and looked up at the sky. It was a typical overcast spring day on the fens. To add to the gloom, a thick sea mist had rolled in from the east. It seemed to suck the heat out of the air as it drifted over the reeds. The trickle charger did not work well under these conditions, so he needed to conserve energy. It had been his intention to change location, never spending more than one night in the same place, but these were treacherous conditions at the best of times. This pea-souper made any attempt to move from Hill 16 foolhardy in the extreme. He would sit this one out.

* * * * *

'Mister Cumbor, so nice to meet you. Seth has told me so much about you.'

Harry Cumbor stood on the doorstep of his thatched cottage in the gruesomely named Cotswold village of Lower Slaughter. A wiry, wizened old curmudgeon, his decades of trekking through jungles and across snow caps had given him muscles like wire rope and leathery skin as thick as rhino hide. He eyed up the young Asian man in front of him with suspicion.

'Jake, you say? Your name is Jake? I don't think Seth has spoken of you. You are from – where?'

'I am at college with Seth, at Norwich. He said I should pop in and say hello from him as I was passing by Oxford.'

The young man raised his voice. Harry hated it when people treated him like an old man. His 80th birthday might be just weeks away, but he wasn't going deaf. This boy was beginning to get on his wick. Why had his nephew foisted this irritating person on him? It was not like Seth at all, but he must be polite. The student was foreign after all and he did not wish to be labelled a racist.

'Would you like some tea? I usually have elevenses about now, Jake. Is Jake your actual name? You don't seem to be from around these parts – as they say in the Westerns.'

'No, Mister Cumbor, you are so observant. I am from China, from Hong Kong. My name? I don't think you would be able to pronounce it.'

They both laughed.

'Tea would be good. No milk, if you please.'

Harry moved off towards the kitchen while the young gang member scanned the room looking for anything that might help him in his quest. This was one of his first assignments and he did not wish to disappoint. The room was cluttered, the cramped feeling exacerbated by the low ceiling and heavy window frames around small glass panes. There were photographs everywhere. Harry on a mountaintop, Harry in a jungle, Harry with Seth.

Harry came back into the room and put the tea down in front of Jake.

'Thank you, Mister Cumbor. I see your picture with Seth; where was that taken?'

'That was only last year on his 21st birthday.'

'Ah yes, big celebration. Many presents.'

'Yes, I bought him a phone.'

'You bought him a mobile phone?'

Tao seemed distinctly underwhelmed by the revelation. Harry felt compelled to explain. 'Ah, but not just any mobile phone, but a satellite mobile phone, just like this one.'

He got up and pulled out what looked for all the world like a cross between an old Nokia handset and a walkie-talkie.

'The very latest, so the man in the shop told me.'

'Can you call him on it?'

'Well, I don't know. Let's give it a try.'

He switched on the unit and punched in Seth's name. After a moment a recorded message came back: *Your call could not be connected at this time.*

The user may have their unit powered off. Please try again later.' He did not leave a message.

In the street, the 4 × 4 with the blacked out windows monitored the call and relayed the number to the newly arrived search squad from Shanghai. If Whitten turned his unit on, they would have him.

Jake drank his tea, thanked Harry and bade him farewell.

'When I see Seth again, I will tell him that you called.'

'Please do, Mister Cumbor.'

They shook hands and Jake walked off down the road and out of sight before getting into the waiting RV.

'Well done, Tao. Now we can trace him with the sat. phone. You must let Franks know Cumbor called him. I sense we will soon be catching up with Mister Whitten.'

* * * * *

'He has made a call, Ma'am.'

'Fantastic! How long will it take to triangulate his position?'

'Already done, but we have a problem: thick fog is preventing the chopper taking off. The weather guys are saying a day, maybe two, before it clears.'

'Sod the chopper. Get cars out there now. I want this little prick brought in today.'

'But Ma'am—'

'Don't screw me around. Get on with it!'

'— he's in the middle of Strumpshaw fen. We need tracker dogs if we are to go after him today.'

'Fuck!'

Franks could not believe her bad luck. Pressure was being brought to bear from a source other than Sharkey. There was a sinister overtone to this new group. For one, they had not only established that Whitten had a satellite phone – a fact of which Franks had been blissfully unaware – and they had somehow managed to obtain its number. Clearly this academic had contacts much wider than off duty police officers doing a bit of a nixer.

Franks had a bad feeling about this. There was much more to this search than met the eye. The resources being employed to track down some two-bit hacker were totally disproportionate and with the surprise involvement of the Chinaman, the whole thing had gone international. She was now beginning to be concerned about her own position.

While the fortuitous call from the Met. had given some legitimacy to what she was doing, her use of a police chopper was going to raise eyebrows in Finance. Did the search for a single missing person, who, so far as anyone in the Force knew, had committed no crime, really warrant the use of so many vehicles and so much officer overtime? She could see this coming back to haunt her.

'Get the dogs out there and fast. I want this guy found.'

She was prepared to throw everything at this

to get it over with and let the devil take the hind-most.

* * * * *

Two hours had gone by since Seth had initiated the searches. The fog was as thick as ever and he was bored and cold. He fired up the sat. phone and made a data connection. Nothing further had come out of the email search but there was an interesting link that had been pulled up on the Internet search. It was to do with Professor Yat-sen's meteoric rise to prominence. It all seemed to hinge on his research on the extraction of some rare earth metal from a mineral called Bastnäsite – pretty esoteric stuff. What did that have to do with Yat-sen's current work in environmental research?

Three things happened at once. Away in the distance Seth caught the faint sound of a dog barking. It deflected his attention momentarily from the next line of the Yat-sen article, which described the aforementioned rare earth metal as lanthanum. Lanthanum? Hmm, he knew something about lanthanum, now what was it? And there was a small icon on the sat. phone that was alerting him to something. He selected it – 'missed call' – what the hell? Who in God's name had been calling his sat. phone? Nobody knew he had one. Then his brain exploded in a fireball of realisations. That wasn't a dog – that was several dogs and they were heading his way. Whoever had called his sat. phone had given away his position and lanthanum was an essential ingredient of the permanent magnets in wind turbines and 95 per cent of that lanthanum came from China. That was it. That was the link with Yat-sen and the funds to Norwich.

But all that would have to wait because just now he had to save his life.

CHAPTER 8

'Tyson, Tyson, hold on there, boy.'

The dog team had spent the day splashing through the fringes of the marshlands. This was a fool's errand, but more than that, someone could drown out here. The conditions were the worst Officer Higginbottom had encountered in more than 20 years with the force. He could barely see his hand in front of his face. They were in a trackless marsh. While the dogs did not need to see to follow the trail, the handlers did if they were to avoid a major human tragedy.

What he did not understand was the urgency attached to apprehending this particular fugitive. He had been told in no uncertain terms that if he valued his job with the dog squad which he did – he was not to come back until he had in his clutches one Seth Whitten, student and sometime hacker of sensitive information from the computers of Norwich University. If Whitten had been some crazed axe murderer, there might have been some justification, but a limp-wristed computer geek. *Give me a break!* But orders were orders and they pressed on into the fen.

A tee-shirt of the suspect had been given to the dogs to sniff and they had picked up a strong scent leading from the station at Buckenham. They had been lucky in that there had been no rain in the preceding few days but their luck ran out shortly after entering the fen. The dogs quickly lost the scent and began sniffing around aimlessly in the fog.

To have begun this search in the present conditions with just dogs would have been totally foolhardy but Higginbottom did have one ace up his sleeve, a very precise latitude and longitude of 52 degree 35 minutes 43.32 seconds north and 1 degree 27 minutes 33.63 seconds east respectively. No doubt when Whitten heard them coming he would make a run for it. That's when the dogs would really come into their own.

'Stay tight, men, we don't want to lose anyone in this shit.'

While Higginbottom had been a dog handler for most of his working life, he was a relative newcomer to East Anglia. On secondment from the Derbyshire force, his experience was more in the line of tracking down lost hill walkers and mountaineers, a number of whose lives he had saved, with medals to prove it.

This stinking bog-land was an altogether different matter. You couldn't track a scent in water and the reed beds appeared to have no paths whatsoever. The further they moved into the mire and away from solid ground, the deeper the water got. It was not long before one of his officers was in over his head, quite literally.

'Get him out; be careful not to go in with him, you clowns!'

'Sarge, this is a fooking waste of time. I'm covered in crap and I can't see a bleedin' thing.'

The rubber gasket on the neck of Officer Penrose's dry suit had done its job and kept the worst excesses of his underwater adventure from completely ruining his day. He wiped the mud from his eyes, his short wet hair matted with rotting black reed fronds, giving him the appearance of a poorly made up bog monster from some trashy B movie.

'You feckless waster, stay on the path and will someone get us a bearing on that sat. phone location?'

Within less than 100m, they came to a dead end. The route to their quarry was now barred by open water, and due to the thickness of the fog Higginbottom was unable to discern where or even if there was dry land on the other side.

'We need boats. Will someone get on the radio and get me some boats out here?'

This was a shambles. His inexperience of the conditions was all too clear, not only to himself but to the men around him. He could hear mutterings and knew he was losing what little respect he had left. This was not his finest hour; and by the time the boats arrived it would be getting dark. He was calling off the search, he would take his chances with Lady Franks; she was not his boss, just a blow in from the Met. She would be gone soon and then they could all get back to the quiet life. He swallowed hard as he made the call.

Franks wasn't pleased. 'Oh Jesus, give me strength. Who employed you, Shit for Brains? Do I have to go out there and apprehend this prick myself?'

Franks knew the aborted search would have no doubt alerted Whitten to the fact that they knew where he was. If he was half the man she thought he was, he would have put two and two together and realised that it was the use of his sat. phone that had given away his position. He would not use that again and if she did not move fast, he could be out of her reach and the Chinaman would not be pleased.

'I want blocks on all roads leading out of Norwich. I want watches kept on all stations within 10 miles of his location. I want it now, dammit!'

* * * * *

The search had not come from the direction Seth had expected. He had anticipated a broad search, a helicopter sweep over tens of square miles, something general. That he could evade, but a specific targeted search directly on his location in the marsh, that he had not planned for. There was only one possible way they could have located him and that was the sat. phone. It was now virtually useless, except in an absolute emergency. His link to the Internet was gone. He needed to get out of the fen. In an instant it had gone from benign fortress to treacherous prison. With his Tissot T-Touch and his hand-drawn map, he would have to navigate his way through the marsh to open water and the River Yare.

The backlight on Seth's watch lit up the magnetic compass as he negotiated the soft pathways between his carefully prepared (and now redundant) hides and out to Hill 25 on the farthest reach of the fen. He knew the police would be waiting for him if he tried to make it straight back to the station.

The noise of the dogs had begun to abate after just 45 minutes. Perhaps his faith in the impregnable nature of the marsh was not misplaced. Probably a combination of loss of scent and the fog had led the pursuit team to rethink their methods. Smart move. Even with his local knowledge and detailed maps, Seth was finding it difficult to navigate the treacherous conditions.

Standing on Hill 25, he was definitely where he should be; now for a leap into the great unknown. Ahead of him, for as far as he could see through the fog, was open water: a meandering bend of the river. This area of East Anglia was so flat that the flow of the water was almost imperceptible. The river wound its way, twisting and turning so much that on occasions it looped back on itself. But its general heading was always to the sea and its direction and speed of flow suited Seth perfectly.

Leaving the sleeping bag inside the bivvy bag, he screwed up the open end and began to blow.

Within five minutes, he was light-headed. The orange plastic survival sack began to grow. He prayed that he had not punctured it over the three nights he had slept in the reeds. When he had brought it with him from the lock-up with the rest of his survival gear, it had still been in its original plastic pouch – he had never had an occasion to use it. After 15 minutes of blowing and stopping, blowing and stopping, he had a large, squishy, orange sausage, 6ft long and 2ft 6 inches wide. This was to be his bivvy bag 'boat'.

Taking four lengths of driftwood he had collected, he lashed them together with reed fronds to make a rough rectangular frame of wood. While giving some buoyancy, it was mainly needed to keep the sleeping bag in place as it weighed down the underside of the bivvy, forming an ever so crude keel. Those tedious evenings spent at the scout hall and fun weekends camping out in the woods had finally paid off – dib dib dib.

With all the electronics stuffed in the Ziploc bags strapped to his back, Seth laid the makeshift craft on the water and gingerly straddled the 'boat', prostrating himself along its length to keep the centre of gravity as low as possible. He had deliberately underinflated the bag to allow him to sink as close to the surface of the river as possible without getting his body wet.

His legs and arms dangled in the water on either side. This could not be helped; so long as he kept his torso and head dry, he should be able to retain a high enough core body temperature to avoid hyperthermia as the river drew heat relentlessly from his exposed appendages. The late spring water temperature in the fens rarely fell below 15° C. Even so, he needed to be off the water within two hours or his muscles would start to spasm and he would be unable to give any guidance to the craft. To add to his woes, it was getting dark and the air temperature was beginning to fall.

While the river flowed at approximately 4 miles an hour, two hours of drifting would take him only about 4 miles from his current position due to the nature of its meanderings. But it was this very meandering that Seth was relying on to enable him to make it back to shore and not be taken out to sea.

On the inside bend of each loop in the river, the water slowed down dramatically, dropping any silt it was carrying and building up a shallow muddy beach. In two hours' time he would paddle towards the north shore, knowing that he would eventually hit one of these points. Setting his watch, he pushed himself off into midstream and began the count down. It was going to be a slow journey.

While the wind had dropped as the sun set, there was still a slight offshore breeze that carried the voices of the search party as they began to fan out, setting up a perimeter along the bank to catch Seth if he tried to return to dry land. The standard operating procedure in such a man hunt was a 4 mile radius from point of last contact. Four miles an hour was the theoretical maximum speed a person could travel over rough ground. Four miles would put Seth's projected return to shore right at the outer limits of the search party. He hoped the river was running a little faster today.

* * * * *

As night closed in, Higginbottom's morale sank even lower. The good news was that the fog was lifting and they would soon have a chopper in the air. The bad news was that there had been not a sniff of their quarry. It would be all too easy for him, in the dark, to slip between the men lining the perimeter.

Higginbottom felt his only hope was that Seth had chosen to sit tight for the night somewhere in the marsh. If he had, he was done for. The police helicopter was night-flight capable and its main search weapon was a thermal imaging camera. In a cold, wet marsh, a hot human body would stand out like a Roman candle. But there was a gnawing sense of doom that had been welling up since the beginning of the search. He felt out of his depth, literally and metaphorically. Give him the cold bare moorlands of Bleaklow. You could stick this bog-land where the monkey stuffed his nuts.

At last Higginbottom heard the drone of the helicopter and he could just make out the powerful searchlight through the slowly retreating fog. Fortunately, the helipad was further inland from where the fog had cleared first. Within minutes, the thermal camera would penetrate the darkness and give them a temperature image of the marsh, starting from the triangulated GPS location of the sat. phone. His spirits started to rise. There was no way Whitten could have got back onto shore without alerting the dogs. The only way he could have possibly evaded them was by boat and there was no way he could have carted a boat into the heart of the fen.

* * * * *

Seth could hear the helicopter away over to the west. No doubt it would concentrate its initial search around Hill 16. He calculated he was just short of 4 miles away from that position and still drifting east. He needed to get to shore fast and lose himself near a heat source. There was no way the 'copter could see him through the dark and fog. It must be equipped with thermal imaging – he needed to blend in.

Using his hands, he began to paddle to shore. He had kept his arms and legs still for nearly two hours. While this made for excruciating pain when he began to move them again, it guaranteed the minimum loss of heat since his body would have very quickly reduced the blood flow to his extremities as the heat drained away into the river. Any attempt to flex them or keep them moving would only have opened up the blood vessels again, drawing away precious heat from his core. Pain seared through his arms and legs as he began his slow direction change, but the adrenalin that had surged through him at the sound of the chopper was like a boost of nitro in his veins, energising what was, up to that moment, a body about as energetic as a boa constrictor in the Arctic.

It was not long before he heard the faint hiss of the underside of the inflated bag as it scraped along the bottom of the gently shelving bed of the river on a tight left turn, bringing him within a spit of the shore. He tried to slide silently into the water but his hours lying prone on a cold plastic bag in a fog bank had left him uncoordinated and weak kneed. His chest hit the water with a smack, legs sank thigh deep into the mud as he grabbed out wildly to hold onto the bivvy bag before it floated away. He could not have made more noise if he had launched himself off a high diving board and belly flopped into a tin bath.

'Did you hear that?'

A voice rang out, not 100 yards away.

'No, what was it?'

'I don't know. I just thought I heard something out there towards the river.'

Within seconds the voices were drowned out by the sound of the helicopter.

Seth could feel the downdraft of the rotor blades; he could just about make out the reed beds on the bank through the retreating fog. It felt like a scene from a National Geographic documentary, the caribou trying to cross the mud flats to get away from the hunters, eventually grinding to a halt, mud up to its belly caught in the cross hairs of the marksman, but in Seth's case, he did not think his hunters were packing tranquiliser darts – something more lethal, no doubt. But he didn't care. He was utterly exhausted, his energy levels so low he did not have the strength to lift even one foot out of the clawing mud, sucking at his calves. All his senses were overwhelmed by the cold, the fog and the deafening noise of those damned rotor blades. Why didn't they get on with it?

'Copter to base, 'copter to base, the fen is clear; I say again the fen is clear. Eastern ground search team spotted. No heat signatures beyond this point. Awaiting instructions.'

Higginbottom's heart sank. This was his last hope. How could his quarry have so easily eluded his search team? This was a student-type nerd, not bloody James Bond. Unless Q had come and spirited him away in a mini submarine, he could not fathom how he could possibly have got out of the swamp. 'Run the search again, from west to east. Extend the search area south; he must have crossed the river. Assume he is using a boat   find him.'

As the chopper moved away, the search team below wiped the mud off their faces.

'Why did that bastard sky jockey have to come in so low? As if life isn't bad enough for us down here, he has to make it worse by stirring up the mud. Well, fuck him and the horse he road in on!'

Being at the end of the search line, Carson and Lloyd, or Cagney and Lacey, as they were derogatively known back at the police station, had drawn the short straw. They were at the furthest reach from search central, based at Buckenham. They were 4 miles from hot coffee, 4 miles from a nice warm room and four hours from a ride home.

'Didn't you say you heard something?'

'I don't know. Who gives a shit? If the chopper can't find this fucker, how are we supposed to? Let's get out of this water and wait for the pickup. I'm not walking another step.'

Seth held his breath. They had come within 50ft of where he lay. He was convinced that the helicopter had found him and would direct the ground team to his position. But the chopper left and, by the conversation of the two grunts on the bank, it was clear that they were unaware of him. But the infrared camera must have picked him up. He was a big, bright infrared signal in a very cold, dark mass of water; how could they possibly have missed him?

And then it dawned, the pilot would have seen three heat signatures, roughly 50ft apart. He must have assumed that Seth was part of the search team. And as any military strategist would tell you, 'assumption is the mother of all fuckups'. *Well,* Seth thought, *Amen to that.* Perhaps he would live to fight another day, but he would have to get out of the water, which was literally draining his life away.

The search team had moved back to the bank but was still no more than 100ft away. If Seth was to do anything, he would have to do it very quietly. There was a small patch of mud tantalisingly close. The river was very slightly tidal at this point, no more than a few inches every 12 hours but just enough to leave this mud bank exposed at low water. Reaching under the bivvy bag boat, Seth pulled out the driftwood frame. With fingers trembling from the cold, he managed to detach the four lengths of wood from each other and, using the two longer sticks like ski poles, he began to lever his legs out of the ooze. Stepping forward on his right leg, the water rushed in to fill the space vacated by his right foot. As he progressed, his feet sank once again into the mud, but less deeply each time since the ground became more solid the closer he got to the bank. Every step was a supreme effort of will and a test of his ability to breathe quietly while undergoing extreme exertion.

It took Seth 15 minutes to travel less than 20ft He fell to his knees on the mud bank and, using one of the 'ski poles', fished out the bivvy bag that was beached in the shallow water of the river bend. In the damp foggy air, his wet body began to shake uncontrollably. If he did not get warm soon, hypothermia would set in and the environment, the blessed environment, would do to him what his pursuers could not.

Using the pen knife from his cycle pouch, he cut the bindings on the neck of the bivvy bag, nicking his finger as he did so. The blood made the process a sticky but painless affair, as his hands had long ago lost any feeling. The air soughed out of the bag but the plastic itself made a noise like the opening of a crisp packet in a cinema. He expected the boys in blue to come pounding through the marsh to arrest him but he was reassured by the grunting conversation between the two rocket scientists as they held station.

Seth retrieved his sleeping bag from the now deflated bivvy bag and, using it as a ground sheet; he unrolled the mercifully dry contents on top. With agonising slowness he removed his soaking wet clothes. Sky clad, he climbed into the sleeping bag, pulling the drawstring tight, allowing himself just a small ingress of fresh air. His muscles began to relax and the spasms started to leave his body. He could hear an occasional muffled expletive from his honour guard. If they only knew the source of their overtime was lying less than 80 feet away – he would have laughed, if he could have summoned up the energy.

Sleep came in an instant, only to be shattered a few minutes later by the shrieking pain that wracked his body as the feeling began to return to his extremities; stuffing the lining of his cocoon into his mouth was the only way to suppress the compulsion to cry out loud. He felt a cooling in his chest as the capillaries in his fingers and toes opened up and began to allow cold blood to be circulated back into the body core. This had been fatal for many rescued skiers, as the rush of cold blood brought on a heart attack in those less energetic and of advanced years who might have ventured out onto the slopes. This fate was not about to befall Seth but there was a part of him that would have dearly welcomed death if it would only put an end to this excruciating pain.

The radio squawked and the officers jumped. They had perched themselves on an old sleeper lying by the railways tracks and had nodded off.

'Carson, are you hearing me? Carson, you old bastard, get yourselves moving. The search radius has been widened; I want you another mile downriver in 15 minutes. Call me when you get there and keep your eyes peeled.'

'Oh Jesus, this is a fucking nightmare! Yes, sarge, will do.'

The two officers began to make their way along the rough path running down the side of the railway track as it made its closest approach to the marsh.

'I'm telling you, if I catch the little sod, I won't be taking prisoners; I'll drown the fucker myself.'

The commotion startled Seth out of his slumbers. He heard the crunch of boots on gravel as the two set off at a fast pace downriver. This was his opportunity to escape, but he was so fatigued he could barely move…

* * * * *

Higginbottom had spoken again to Franks. He had attempted to call off the search but she was having none of it.

'Get your lazy, good-for-nothing squad off their fat arses and bring me Whitten. I don't care how long it takes – it could take all night for all I care but bring him to me.'

Franks was beginning to despair. The Chinaman had been on again, looking for an update.

'It is now eight hours since we gave you Mr Whitten's location – you have him?'

His voice was at once polite but menacing. He had that annoying Oriental habit of asking questions while making a statement. She felt the pressure. It was not just the money that was at stake, her own professional pride had taken a beating. She was being outmanoeuvred by an ingénue. She was the specialist – this is what she did. Whitten was a computer hacker; some wanker who knew his way around a hard drive but should not have been capable of outwitting one of Her Majesty's finest.

'Should you fail to find Mr Whitten by noon today, I am afraid that my employer has informed me that he will no longer need your services. Goodbye, Inspector.'

He gave her no opportunity to explain, no opportunity to negotiate an extended time frame. She had not slept for 24 hours and exhaustion was beginning to set in. She needed to get some shut-eye. Charlie Chan was not going to tell her when she could call off the search. Since the Commander had contacted her, this had become an official police investigation, no longer a bit of work on the side. He could go fuck himself! She curled up on the office couch. Let's see what the morning would bring.

CHAPTER 9

Daylight flooded the sleeping bag.
'Oh Christ!'
He looked at his watch – it was 5 am. He peered from his nest and was greeted by a spectacular sunrise and a cloudless fog-free day. He could see for miles – and so could his would-be captors. Seth was out of his bag and into the cool morning air in a flash – literally, stark, bollock naked. A pile of bloody, muddy rags masqueraded as his clothes – what to do?

He wrung the worst of the wet out of each item. There was some warmth in the sun as it hung low in the sky. It could be one of those rare occasions – a bright spring day on Strumpshaw. Just what he needed if he was to dry off his kit as he made his way out of this godforsaken fen. Once again, he could hear barking away in the distance. They must be running another sweep downriver. The dogs sounded a long way off and did not seem to be moving fast. With no scent to follow, their handlers were searching more in hope than expectation.

* * * * *

Connie and Randolph had spent the night in Seth's flat, Connie on the bed and Randolph on the sofa. They woke early.

'We must do something. Seth is out there, maybe injured, maybe dead, and we are just sitting here.'

'But sometimes, Connie, it is best, as the great man, said, "When you don't know what to do, do nothing." If we were to rush around the countryside searching for him at random, we might miss a call from him here or information from Inspector Franks.'

'I don't trust that woman. I think she is more interested in nailing him for distributing the Climategate e-mails than she is in making sure he comes home safe. Anyway, I don't think she is telling us all she knows.'

'But then, darling, neither are we telling her all we know, or at least suspect.'

Randolph had discovered over his many years in sticky situations that one of the toughest things to do, when you are under pressure to act, is nothing. And so often he had found it to be the most productive form of action, or inaction, depending on which way you looked at it. Inaction gave time for reasoned thought; it put the brakes on, stopping you making the bad decisions in the short term. Maybe running round Norwich sticking up missing person notices, offering a reward for the safe return of one Seth Whitten would generate some leads and make them feel that they were being productive, but more likely it would smoke out a few kooks or conmen, interested in making a quick buck – there was no benefit in being a busy fool.

If they couldn't go hunting for Seth physically, then they could certainly put their time to good use. Randolph had spent the previous day slaving over a hot phone. He had called in every favour from every contact he had, in both the UK and Ireland – and he had quite a few. His time spent in the Irish military had given him access at the highest level throughout these islands but it had availed him nothing.

Connie set about trawling the web for any information linking global warming, Professor Yat-sen and China. Seth seemed to have been obsessed by Yat-sen and she hoped that her internet searches might shine a light on whether this had some bearing on Seth's disappearance. But after days of digging all they came up with were some conflicting accounts of China's commitment to green energy. On the one hand, China was the world's foremost supplier of wind turbines to the West and on the other; they were opening one new coal-fired power station, the size of Drax B, every week, and running them on dirty, gritty, high sulphur brown coals from open-cast strip mines to boot. But so what? China was hypocritical when it came to industry *v*. the environment.

In a related article, a British government contract for wind turbines worth over $24 billion appeared to be going to China Iron and Steel Inc. in contravention of a tendering process Maybe that was a link with Yat-sen. Who could tell?

In the end Connie had put in a salving phone call to Franks' office but all it had elicited was the predictable response that they were 'following up on a number of leads and will call if there are any developments'.

'Come on, Connie, let's get out of here. You said there was a lake on the campus – a stiff walk might help clear our heads before breakfast.'

It was becoming clear that if Seth was to be found, they were going to have to do it themselves.

* * * * *

Is there anything more unpleasant than putting on cold wet clothes? Seth decided that at this moment in time there was not. A poke in the eye with a sharp stick would have been preferable, but the fastest way to dry his clothes was to wear them, with the added bonus of reducing his chances of being arrested for streaking, if not for computer hacking. He shivered in the early morning light; with his bag strapped to his back, he began a commando crawl through the reeds towards the railway line.

At the edge of the marsh he saw evidence of his two night-time companions: cigarette butts, sweet papers and sandwich bags. What did they teach these guys at Police College? Certainly nothing on environmentalism. His ingrained respect for the countryside almost had him tidying up the mess but sense prevailed and instead he relieved himself over the litter. He was sure the dogs would pick up his scent as he crossed from the reeds to the railway tracks. His hope was that the pungent smell of urine mixed in with the cigarette butts and associated police detritus would not only confuse the animals, but lead his trackers to believe that it was their dirty colleagues who had generated the scent.

Seth intended his own scent trail to begin and end almost immediately, in the hope that they would move on down the track and not figure out what had actually happened; but for his plan to work, he needed a train, a very specific train – in fact, the 05:10 from Norwich to Great Yarmouth.

Seth had travelled on this nearly empty train on a number of occasions during his studies. It was not really a scheduled run. There was no way it could make any money at that time in the morning with the passenger load in single figures. Its main function was the repositioning of the last train out of Great Yarmouth from the night before. This train would become the 06:00 commuter service out of Great Yarmouth, getting into Norwich at 06:30, the first of a series of half-hourly shuttles back and forth during the morning rush hour. At 05:25 the East Midlands Diesel would slow to a crawl as it approached the unmanned crossing at Polkey's Mill.

Polkey's Mill and Steam Pump was something of a tourist attraction, with its beautifully restored 19th century windmill, nestling on the banks of the River Yare. But like human flypaper, the lure of the windmill could be the kiss of death for the unwary traveller. Yes, there was the phone to ring the station and check if any trains were due; yes, there were numerous signs warning of the danger of oncoming trains at the un-gated crossing; but after three fatal accidents and numerous near misses, the trains approaching the crossing were now required to slow down to give the human lemmings time to scuttle away.

By the time Seth reached the embankment, he could already hear the screech of metal on metal as the inertia of the slowing train caused the wheels to slip on the rails. As he scrambled up the gravel bank, he was pleased to see that the only barrier to the single-line track was a scrubby hedge, which was holey enough not to impede his run, while at the same time providing him with just the right amount of cover to prevent the driver from seeing his attempt to board. The train was a two-carriage unit with a cab at either end, making it possible to be driven in either direction. A small cow catcher was fitted to deflect any obstacles on the track and Seth was counting on it to provide him with a platform onto which he could jump as the train slithered past. As he prepared to make his dash across the 10ft between the hedge and the carriage, the squealing brakes fell silent and the engine began to speed up again.

It was now or never! He slipped and stumbled across the oil-spattered stones of the rail bed and lunged for the back of the receding train. His right hand grabbed a tubular bar on the vertical face below the driver's window. He stepped onto the flared edge of the cow catcher but the train was now moving so fast that it almost pulled his shoulder out of its socket. His trainers, still wet from the hours spent soaking in the Yare, slipped on the sloping painted surface of the plough blade and his left arm flailed as he tried to get another hand hold. The cow catcher, which had in his mind's eye been a large safe platform for him to ride on into Great Yarmouth, was in fact a rather slim-angled, slippery blade that did not provide him with the haven he had been expecting.

As he swung wildly away from the back of the train, he was blown back in by the slip stream as the coaches gathered pace. His left hand closed around the handle of the driver's door set into the front of the carriage and he almost lost his grip as the handle moved down under his grasp and the door clicked open. He was at once elated that the door was unlocked and astounded at the health and safety implications of such a security lapse. He tumbled inside, slamming the door behind him.

At the front of the train a red warning light briefly lit up on the instrument panel. The train driver gave the offending bulb a hefty wallop with his not insubstantial fist, frowned and then smiled in satisfaction as it flickered out. Another problem-free day was beginning on the 'milk and honey line'.

Seth crawled along the floor of the driver's cab and peeped through the glass of the connecting door to the passenger section. His luck was in – it was empty. He twisted the handle – his luck was out: the connecting door was locked; maybe health and safety would not be so upset after all. He resigned himself to spending the final 15 minutes of his journey in the relative comfort of the floor of the cab and the delicious warmth of the train's heating system. Seth stripped down to his shorts and put his still damp clothing over the heating vents on either side of the carriage. He unfurled his trusty bivvy bag, forming a tent over one of the vents, and luxuriated in the hot atmosphere trapped inside. His runners began to steam – the smell was mighty.

Within minutes, the train was slowing again for a brief stop at the tiny, one-platform Berney Arms station. It was less than two years since Seth had first laid eyes on Berney Arms. Like so many places on this largely featureless landscape, it was named after a local mill. Much to the annoyance of his fellow travellers, he had laughed out loud as the train had drawn to a halt, the driver warning that anyone wishing to exit should do so from the front carriage. The reason for the safety instruction was all too clear as the platform, if one could call it that was less than the length of a single carriage.

Its black cinder path was dotted with weeds, but this was not the target of Seth's mirth; it was reserved for the platform's shelter, a brown clapperboard affair, barely the width of a portly gent, with standing room for just three people shoulder to shoulder. With its pointy roof and tiny windows set in each wall, seen from the right it looked for all the world like a Buckingham Palace sentry box, but one built by someone with a penchant for garden sheds.

Seth waited for the driver's safety warning, but as no one got off or on he had obviously decided on this occasion to give it a miss. Next stop Yarmouth. Staying under the bright orange bivvy bag, Seth was confident that should anyone chance to look into the rear cab, they would assume the bundle of brightly coloured material was some discarded high visibility clothing. He was particularly keen not to be seen exiting the train. He did not want to arouse any suspicions that might encourage his pursuers to redirect their search away from the fens. The longer they wasted their time with that particular activity, the more chance he had to put significant distance between himself and the police. If only he could put the clock back, rein in his impetuous arrogance. He wished he'd listened to Connie.

Connie! He had not thought of her in hours. What was wrong with him? The sun rose and set for Connie; she must be frantic with worry. How could he do this to her? He must send a message letting her know that he was OK. The sat. phone was an absolute no-no. He needed to use some method that would not give away his location but would make it clear to Connie, and only Connie, that he was alright. As the train pulled into Yarmouth station, he began to formulate a plan.

CHAPTER 10

This was the third time Higginbottom had led the dog team along the shore line to the 4 mile extreme of the search pattern. At first light he had extended the search radius by 1 mile – he was desperate. He had sent Cagney and Lacey on down the track and was now maybe 2 miles behind them. His own dog, Rufus, was on a long leash. It kept getting tangled in the light scrub that lay between his team and the railway line. The first train of the day had past him maybe half an hour earlier, heading towards Yarmouth. He would dearly have loved to be on it. It was not the physical tiredness that was getting to him; it was the utter tedium of trailing up and down the same path, maintaining a perimeter against someone he was sure was long gone. If the helicopter with infrared cameras could not find this joker, then what hope had he?

While the officer's mind wandered, Rufus set off on another false trail. He had found the night-time resting place of the two constables who had been sent off to extend the perimeter. Higginbottom saw litter and fag ends everywhere – he really would have to have a word with them about that.

Rufus had his nose in the fag ends. One of the men had obviously taken a leak at this spot. He did not need the dog to tell him that, filthy bastards! It was at this point that Rufus took off at right angles to the path heading towards the railway tracks. He had picked up a scent. Within a few yards of the path the leash again became tangled in briars. Higginbottom released his collar clip and gave the dog its head – it made straight for the tracks. With his heart pounding, Higginbottom called to the rest of the team to follow as he tore after the dog. A short run up the gravel bank and he was onto the lines. Rufus was circling, a sure sign he had lost the scent. He ran down the track a short way and then back to his master.

Higginbottom surveyed the scene and took a few moments to gather his thoughts. What was he dealing with here? Was Whitten Rambo or was he, as the sergeant was beginning to suspect, a train spotter who believed too many old wives' tales about being able to put a tracking dog off a scent by urinating to cover his trail.

'Double back and search the marsh on the other side of the track – quickly!'

Maybe at last he would have some good news for Sturmführer Franks.

* * * * *

'Inspector, he caught the 05:10 from Norwich to Great Yarmouth.'

'What the hell! How in God's name did he do that? The stations are covered.'

'We don't think he used a station, Ma'am. The train slows before an unmanned crossing near the point he left the marsh. There is evidence he accessed the rear cab of the train and exited at Great Yarmouth station. We are checking CCTV now.'

'Good work. Higginbottom, good work.'

At last a little bit of good news, but they had missed him by minutes. By Christ this one was a slippery little bugger, but he did make mistakes. Yarmouth was no metropolis but like most ports in England, it was festooned with CCTV cameras and the pursuit was only half an hour behind him.

* * * * *

Seth, now dressed in the warm and slightly less damp clothing, his runners still squelching a little as he walked, gathered his belongings. Before the train reached the platform, it had to slow down as it crossed the points in front of the now defunct 'Yarmouth Vaux' signal box, its name paying homage to Yarmouth's last remaining great train station, 'Yarmouth Vauxhall'. It was a throwback to the heyday of steam and would not have looked out of place to a Victorian traveller.

As the train clattered over the points and lurched to the left, he prepared to alight. His prime concern was not to be seen by the CCTV cameras on the platform or by any unwelcome observer.

The large two-storey signal box was only 100 yards from the extreme end of platforms 1 and 2 but provided perfect cover from the station and the slip road that potentially overlooked his exit point. In a reverse of his boarding of the train, he opened the driver's door, quickly shutting it behind him while clinging to the grab handle and the handle of the door. On this occasion the train was travelling more slowly, no more than 5 miles an hour, and his drop to the track went without incident.

At the front of the train, the driver was once again irritated to see the rear cab door warning light come on. He gave it a thump, which was swiftly rewarded by the light's extinction. He sat back with satisfaction and pondered whether he should have stuck at his first job as an electrician – he clearly had a knack for fixing electrical faults.

Seth ducked behind the brick wall of the signal box. The railway sleepers smelled pungently of oil laid down over decades. It was not altogether unpleasant and it was definitely preferable to the stifling odour of his sweaty trainers in the confines of the driver's cab. After a quick look round to check that the coast was clear, he scrambled over the wire fence and through the bushes up to the slip road. His destination was the Suspension Bridge, a pub opposite the station building overlooking the confluence of two of Yarmouth's rivers, the Yare and the Waveney, as they became Breydon Water. Being the good student that he was, Seth knew his pubs. And this one opened early to catch the commuter traffic to Norwich.

Keeping low and walking back towards the station, he had good cover with the hedge on one side and large advertising billboards on the other. Finally, with the pub in sight, he dodged out from behind the end of the billboards and crossed over to the central reservation of the dual carriageway that ran into the town centre. Walking as nonchalantly as possible, he sauntered across the two lanes, dodging the gathering traffic and in through the back entrance of the pub.

As he correctly recalled, the Gents was to his immediate left and he walked purposefully into the first stall, locking the door behind him. He collapsed onto the white plastic seat and let out a long sigh. He was almost certain that he had exited the train and entered the pub unobserved. The fresh paper roll in the holder told him that the toilets had been recently cleaned and he would not be disturbed any time soon. For the first time in days he felt safe.

* * * * *

The train rolled smoothly to a halt and the driver turned and removed the key, disabling the cab's controls. He levered his 250lb frame out of the seat and unlocked the connecting door to the passenger carriages. He had had no customers on this journey, a not unusual occurrence on his early shift. He waddled down the aisle of the two carriages, the pockets of his tunic brushing the seats on either side. He really would have to do something about his weight, he thought – but not today. Unlocking the rear cab, which was now to become the front of the train for the return journey, he opened the door and was hit by a powerful smell of feet. Someone had been dossing in his cab. The floor was covered in mud and there were bits of foliage all over the heating grills. He reached for the outside handle and found it was unlocked.

'Fucking cleaners, I'll swing for them! I tell you I'll fucking swing for them,' he roared at no one in particular.

He pushed open the outside door to try to clear the air and sank back into his seat, extracted the *Daily Mail* from his pocket and turned to the sports pages to see how the Canaries had fared the night before. The train was not due to leave for another 10 minutes, so he settled back to savour the 2:1 victory over rivals Nottingham Forest. He became dimly aware of a commotion on the platform – running feet. No need to hurry – it was only 06:57 and he would not be pulling out 'til 07:00. No need to panic, time enough… The door to his cab exploded inwards and a burley police constable grabbed his shoulder, swinging his body round painfully.

'Switch off the engine and order an evacuation of the train. Do it now.'

'What, what…?' His voice trailed off in the face of such aggression.

'Do as I say, then come with me.'

'What 'ave A done? 'Ave done nothin', nothin'

A tell yuh!'

Exasperated, the policeman grabbed the intercom and informed the astonished passengers that the train had been cancelled and to leave in an orderly fashion. With much grumbling and freely expressed resentment, the two carriages slowly emptied and the bemused driver was led away for interrogation.

* * * * *

'Now tell me, Mr Singleton, did you notice anything unusual about the passengers you carried from Norwich to Yarmouth this morning?'

Higginbottom was conducting the interview in the platform coffee shop with a clear view of the train now marooned on platform 1.

'Yes, yes, A did.'

'And what was that, Mr Singleton?'

'Well,' – he leaned forward with a conspiratorial air as he lowered his voice – 'well, yuh' see, they was invisible.'

'What are you talking about?'

'Yo' said there was passengers on ma train this mornin' and am telling you that if there was, then they was bloody invisible, 'cos I never saw 'em.'

This was just great, only the most important interview Higginbottom had ever conducted and he had to get a smart alec. His colleague standing guard at the door smirked and Higginbottom's sphincter tightened at the anticipation of the ridicule he would receive back at the station. The driver was not only a smart alec, he was also bolshy. He had refused to talk to 'Constable Thick Head by the door', as he had been strong armed out of his own cab. As a more senior officer, Higginbottom had been brought in to smooth things over. The driver had just made a fool of him and he knew it, and soon everyone in the local nick would know it. He tried again.

'OK then, did anything unusual happen on the way down from Norwich, anything at all?'

The driver stared down at his hands for a moment as if in thought. Higginbottom looked across at the train. It had been cordoned off with tape and cones and he could see Forensics in their puffy white coveralls crawling all over the driver's cab with their makeup brushes and cameras.

'Yeh, now yu come t'uh mention it, something odd did 'appen. 'Bout a couple of stations back the warnin light for rear cab door come on and then went off again. It did same thing again just as we come int'uh station.'

'Could that mean someone was entering or leaving the rear cab?'

'Yes, it could, it could but train was moving both times and what daft bugger would do that?'

Higginbottom suppressed a smile. Now he was getting somewhere. 'Thick Head' was not looking so cocky. He pressed on.

'This is very important, very important indeed: can you remember precisely at which station you first noticed the light?'

Again the great ponderous beast of a man called upon his few remaining brain cells and set to recalling the incident.

'A think i' t'were just before Polkey's Mill. Yeh, yeh, i' t'were Polkey's Mill 'cos a remember seeing the mill.'

Singleton beamed at him, his little piggy eyes sparkling from behind their protective folds of fat. He had done good, the boy had done good; something to tell his mates in the pub tonight. Who knew, he might even be on the telly.

Higginbottom squeezed the button on his radio.

'That's confirmation, Ma'am, he got on at Polkey's Mill and off at Yarmouth.'

'Great work, Higginbottom, stay where you are. We will have a search team down to you within the hour.'

He threw a triumphant smile in the direction of his bungling colleague as he exited the café. There was no doubt he had overheard the praise from Franks. Now it would be a different story back at the station.

* * * * *

Seth leaned forward and placed his elbows on his knees and pondered. He often had his best ideas when he was sitting on the loo. Something to do with being totally relaxed perhaps, and this had been confirmed in a lecture he once went to by one of the greatest thinkers of modern times – Tony Bussan – so it must be true. And it was now of all times that he needed to come up with a great idea. How was he to get a message to his dearest Connie without giving away his location? He so wanted to use the sat. phone but he knew that was a crazy thought. He also needed to get something to eat. The mere thought of food gave him stomach cramps. It must have been over 24 hours since he had last had a meal. If he did not get an energy boost soon, he would begin to make mistakes. He could not afford to make even one mistake. His life depended on it.

After several minutes in which no eureka moment presented itself, he gave up and left the stall. On approaching the basin to wash his hands, he got a sudden fright as a shocking visage stared back at him from the mirror. *My God what a sight*, he thought taking in the unshaven stubble and mud and blood-streaked matted hair. Thank heavens he had not walked into the bar looking like this. What was he thinking? Clearly his thought processes were already dulled. His priority now was to clean himself up; no one was going to serve a vagrant.

He tried to stick his head in the tiny washbasin, in doing so he banged his eye socket on the tap triggering a surge of uncontrolled rage as he kicked out at the door behind him. It crashed back into the partition between the stalls, splintering the paint as the lock concentrated the force of the blow. His heart stopped at the cacophony of sounds that bounced around the small room. He held his breath, waiting for an investigation by the landlord, but none came. He breathed a sigh of relief. What the hell was wrong with him? He really must get a grip.

He tried again with the washbasin, this time with a little more care. He managed to get the top of his head under the tap and warm water began to wash the filth of the fens from his hair. The water ran black for more than 30 seconds before he started to massage in the hand wash. After sticking his head under the hand dryer for two minutes he took another look in the mirror. Hmm, not bad, thank goodness for short hair. The beard growth would help to disguise him and he decided that the designer stubble look could work for him. He would consult on that subject when he met up again with Connie. After days without thinking of her, now all he could do was think of her; how to get a message to her? He knew her so well – she would be beside herself with worry and boy would he pay for it. At that moment he was not sure which he was most afraid of, the police or the wrath of Connie.

He exited the jacks and opened the door to the lounge bar. The room was empty but for one woman who was just getting up to go to the Ladies, which was on the other side of the bar from the Gents. As she rose, he saw her put her phone into the pocket of a raincoat draped over the chair. She disappeared into the toilets and he quickly walked over to her table, put his hand in the pocket and retrieved her phone. He typed in Connie's mobile number, selected SMS, typed just three words and hit the send key. He replaced the phone in the coat.

Leaving the pub by the front door and making sure that he was not observed, he took the footpath down to the river. Now what he wanted was to put as much distance as he could between himself and that phone.

PART III

It's easier to fool people than to convince them that they have been fooled.

Mark Twain

'The lobbying campaign has succeeded beyond our wildest dreams, Senator. The DOE has really come onboard. We are looking at investment guarantees on green projects in excess of $10 billion. If this can't give us the breakthrough on battery technology, then nothing can.'

Haze relaxed into his brown leather armchair and began to think the unthinkable. His eager young aide had the enthusiasm and belief that he himself sometimes lacked after years of disappointment. Fickle weather systems turned on and off at the whim of the gods with no consideration for the needs of the electricity-consuming public. The failure of the scientific community to come up with a solution to the thorny issue of storing all that potential wind energy was a black cloud over an otherwise very sunny future for the renewables industry.

Could a truly reliable, financially viable mass storage system for electricity be just around the corner? – he dared to dream. Carbon fuel had always had the edge on battery power pound for pound. A tank of gasoline would take a modern fuel-efficient car nearly 800 miles while the latest electric vehicles would scarcely travel 50 miles on a single charge. But all that money, all those billions, surely they would make the difference and lead them into the Promised Land?

CHAPTER 11

Returning to her table, Carolanne Westwood sipped the last of her coffee. She had her tickets and the train to Norwich did not leave 'til 07:30, so she could take her time. At Norwich she would pick up her connection for the express to London. It was always a close run thing but she knew the stations well and had never missed her train before so she was confident that this trip would be no different.

Leaving the pub, she slung the raincoat over her arm. It was a beautiful day but you could never be too sure what English weather might be like. The traffic was building so the underpass provided the quickest route to the station. There was clearly some sort of incident. Numerous police cars with flashing blue lights were parked at all angles outside the main entrance. Inside, her heart sank as she saw the train she normally took from platform 1 cordoned off, but her spirits rose again as an official directed her to the next platform where a relief train was ready to depart. The station was buzzing with police.

On getting seated she was soon in conversation with a fellow traveller delayed from the earlier 07:00 train who imparted the dire news that an escaped convict was on the loose and that tracker dogs were being brought in to hunt him down. Carolanne gave a little shiver and thanked her lucky stars she was getting out of Yarmouth for a few days. Who knew what this guy might do?

* * * * *

Refreshed from their walk, Randolph outlined the situation to Connie while she made breakfast in the kitchen.

'Look, Connie, if Franks had found him, she would be in a lot better mood. Her cooling attitude towards us makes me think she believes we are hiding something – which we are – and if she had found Seth and was holding him incommunicado, she would be a lot more dismissive of us. We wouldn't get the time of day. The only reason she tolerates our calls is that she hopes she might get something out of us that will lead her to him...' Randolph was distracted by the sound of a phone beeping. He walked across to the table where they had plugged in their phones overnight. It was Connie's.

'Any news?' Connie called out as she lifted the fry onto plates.

'It's yours – from an unknown sender. It says "gamma ray bursts"?'

Her mood changed in an instant.

'What is it?'

'He's alive!' She ran over and shouted this in his ear, nearly deafening him.

'But how do you know?'

'Gamma ray bursts – it's what he says to me when I ask him how much he loves me.'

'I don't understand.'

'When I asked him how much he loved me, he used to say "up to the sky" and then he went to an astronomy lecture and learned about these gigantic energy beams that can be seen at the very edge of the visible universe. So now when I ask him how much he loves me, he says, "Up to the gamma ray bursts".' Her face glowed with delight. 'So he's sending a message to say he's OK. Like in code, so if anyone was listening in, they wouldn't know he had contacted me. He's such a smart cookie!'

* * * * *

The man leaned over his dials. The headphones were sticky on his ears. He had spent a very long night listening to nothing but light snoring and the occasional fart. Finally he had something to report. He made some quick notes and then began to run a trace on the young woman's mobile. At the same time he put in a call to Inspector Franks.

'Ma'am, he's made contact with the girlfriend.'

'How?'

'Text message, Ma'am.'

'Do you have his location?'

'Working on that as we speak. Should have it in a few moments.'

'Call me back when you do.'

Franks was not altogether happy. Whitten was nothing if not smart. Making a call to his girlfriend's mobile was a really dumb thing to do. He knew how closely they were tracking him. He must have seen the helicopter, heard the dogs. He had rather ineptly tried to throw them off his scent but had still managed to stay one step ahead of them despite that. She would not get her hopes up yet. The phone rang again.

'We have traced the phone, Ma'am. All the text messages from yesterday were from known friends and relatives of the girl. She received one this morning at 07:00 from a phone registered to a Carolanne Westwood. She is a resident of Great Yarmouth but has no known association with either Whitten or the girl.'

'Where's the phone now?'

'That's the trouble, Ma'am. The phone is moving very quickly between cells. It is either in a very fast car on a motorway—'

'Or on a train. The little bastard's slipped by us and he is on a train. What's the nearest main line to the cell trace?'

'I don't know.'

'Well, bloody well find out! We need to intercept that train before it stops again.'

* * * * *

Carolanne settled back into her first-class seat and gloried in the prospect of having nothing to do for the next hour and three-quarters. It was the one luxury she allowed herself in an otherwise austere lifestyle. She looked around the carriage. She did not like to be in close proximity to the 'great unwashed'. While not of high birth, she considered herself genteel in an otherwise boorish world. The first-class carriage gave her the option of a single or a double seat facing either forward or backward across a table. She, of course, always chose a single seat facing forward. She actually preferred to sit facing backward but after many years of studying passenger habits, she deduced that most people preferred facing forwards and by her taking such a seat she increased her chances of no one sitting opposite her. Once the train was moving and everyone was settled she could swap over and indulge her preference for studying the countryside moving away from rather than toward her.

The express made only one stop on its journey to Liverpool Street Station, the university town of Cambridge with its church spires and ivory towers. On another day, she might have stopped off and taken tea in one of the many stone-clad cafés that dotted the streets and alleyways of this most majestic of cities. But not today. Today she was in a hurry. Her appointment with her editor was at 11:00 and she did not want to keep him waiting. Her particular brand of romantic fiction was rather popular at the moment and Nostrum and Hangle were, for the first time, showing some real interest in her writing. There was even talk of a book tour.

As the carriage filled, Carolanne began to be concerned that someone might sit opposite her. She had her raincoat strategically placed on the empty seat, but while most people were reluctant to ask if the seat was taken, on a full train – needs must. With just a minute to go the aisle had cleared and, looking round, she could see that hers was not the only spare seat and she began to relax. The early start was beginning to catch up on her and she quickly drifted off. The next thing she knew they were pulling into Cambridge. Goodness, she would be in London in no time.

* * * * *

'The phone is on the East Coast Mainline from Norwich to London, Ma'am.'

The man in the van had quickly identified the location of the GSM antenna towers. However, across the flat plane of East Anglia, getting an accurate fix on a phone was difficult due to the relatively large distances between base stations in this rural area. He could at best estimate its location to within half a mile. Initially, this only narrowed things down to either the A14 dual carriageway or the East Coast Mainline, as for over 20 miles these two routes ran parallel, and at an average speed of 75 mph, it could have been on either one of them. Only as the track and the road began to diverge around Newmarket and the approach to Cambridge was he certain that the signal was emanating from the train.

'What is the next stop?'

'Cambridge, Ma'am.'

'I want it stopped before then. I don't want him getting off.'

'I think it's too late for that. Ma'am. According to the timetable, it should be pulling into Cambridge now. Do you want me to detain the train?'

'Of course I want you to detain the fucking train, you imbecile. What do you think we are trying to do here, play pin the tail on the donkey?'

Franks slammed the phone down and screamed out of her office door, 'Get CID in Cambridge to impound the Norwich to London express – don't let anyone get on or off. Do it now!'

The office exploded in a flurry of feverish action. Within minutes a whispering huddle of officers was debating whose responsibility it was to pass on the bad news that the train had already left the station. A junior officer poked his head around the door frame of Franks' office.

'Uh, Ma'am?'

'Yes, yes, what is it?'

'Uh, the London express has already departed…'

He ducked back behind the upright as a stapler whistled by his head. Her accuracy with a stapler was legend but he was ready for her.

'Get me Cambridge CID.'

CHAPTER 12

The squad cars made an incongruous collage against the Romanesque arches of the Cambridge station facade. Twenty officers poured through and onto the platform as the last of the nine coaches of the London express disappeared from sight. The sergeant's radio burst into life.

'This is Inspector Franks of the Metropolitan Police. Stop the London express and get it back onto the platform. Do it quickly or I'll have your badge.'

Within seconds the sergeant was in contact with the signals controller and had brought the Norwich to London express to a grinding halt. After a further 15 minutes of heated argument, phone calls to higher authorities and not a small amount of expletives on both sides, the train began its undignified 2 mile reversing manoeuvre back into Cambridge.

* * * * *

Carolanne had maintained the empty seat after the Cambridge stop and had swapped seats to face backwards for the remainder of the journey. The train had begun to speed up and they were quickly out into the countryside. Suddenly the train lurched, accompanied by a squeal of brakes. Drinks went everywhere and Carolanne was forced back into her seat with the sudden deceleration. All sorts of horrors flew though her mind – perhaps some poor unfortunate had flung themselves onto the line or maybe cattle had escaped and strayed onto the track.

She looked up and down the fields on either side but they were all grain or cabbages. No dairy or beef herds in sight. No, it was most likely a suicide. Oh the poor family! A number of Carolanne's novels had included the terrible subject of lovers taking their own lives, though railways had not played a part in any of the plots – perhaps the next one. A scene began to evolve in her mind but her thoughts were interrupted by the apology from the driver for the delay. He hoped they would be on their way shortly.

Time went by but there was no sign of any movement. Her appointment was now in jeopardy. Ah, thank goodness, the train was moving again. She was surprised at the reaction of the other passengers who let out a collective groan. And then it hit her, of course the train was going backwards; her recent seat switch had confused her sense of direction. Oh no, she was definitely going to miss her appointment now. Delving into her large handbag she retrieved her phone and began to scroll down the address book to find her editor's number and make her apologies.

* * * * *

Franks had taken personal control of the situation. She had directed the officer in charge to clear the platforms and detain everyone on the train.

'What? All 400 of them?'

'Well, all right, all right. Keep them on the train and make sure no one leaves. I want officers on the tracks on both sides.'

Then a call came in from the man in the van.

'He's sent another text, Ma'am.'

'To the girl?'

'No, Ma'am, to a book publisher in Marylebone.'

'What does it say?'

'He is apologising for being late for an appointment.'

Perhaps Whitten had decided to go public with the e-mails through the conventional press.

'Get a gagging order on that publisher. Make sure they do not divulge anything that Whitten might have given them.'

Something was not sitting right here. Why would Whitten go from being such a slippery weasel to a sitting duck? She was beginning to get a bad feeling.

* * * * *

Carolanne watched as the train drew slowly back into Cambridge station. The public address system cautioned the passengers not to try to exit the train as it would be continuing its journey shortly. As the message was being delivered, she noticed the constables on the tracks and on the platform. This was just like at Yarmouth.

A sudden thought struck her. What if the escaped convict had managed to get on her train? He could be in this very carriage. A shiver ran down her spine. As the train shuddered to a halt, the doors opened and a policeman was allocated to each carriage and barred the way for anyone who might want to get off. Nobody did – everyone just wanted to get to London.

Carolanne now relaxed. The proximity of a member of the constabulary made her feel safe. Even if there was a lunatic on the train, any attempt he might make to harm her or any of the other passengers would be quickly dealt with by these fine strong officers.

* * * * *

'OK, where is it? Where's the bloody phone?'

Franks was bawling down the radio at the man in the van.

'It's in the first three coaches. That's the best I can do.'

'Good God, man, with all that equipment, is that as close as you can get? Give me strength. Is there no other way you could narrow it down?'

'Well, we could always ring it.'

There was a pause while she called the sergeant on the platform.

'I want three of your men in each of the first three carriages,' she barked. 'When they are in place, tell me.'

There was hurried activity and then confirmation that everyone was in place. Franks instructed the man in the van to make the call. She held her breath.

* * * * *

Carolanne was thinking about contacting Nostrum and Hangle again. She did not think that the train was going to be going anywhere anytime soon. Just as the thought entered her mind, her phone rang. Who could that be? Maybe her editor was responding to her earlier text. As she picked up her bag to open it, it was forcefully removed from her grasp and a burley policeman leaned over her.

'You had better come quietly, Miss.'

She let out a wail and shrank back into the corner of her seat, at which two officers lifted her bodily and marched her off the train to the total bemusement of the other travellers.

* * * * *

'Now, Miss Westwood – may I call you Carolanne?'

Carolanne cowered in the chair. The interview room smelled of sweat, and not her own. The policeman – if he was a policeman – who sat in front of her across the table, wore civilian clothes. He had taken off his jacket and she could see a dark stain under each armpit. She pulled out a white handkerchief from her pocket and held it to her nose. She had placed two drops of scent on it that morning. This was a ritual she performed whenever she had to leave her house. Body odour repulsed her and on this occasion her little insurance policy had paid dividends.

The officer was speaking to her but she could not understand what he was saying. She could hear him all right but the words seemed jumbled and made no sense. Her heart was beating in her ears and all other sounds appeared muted. She stared back at him and watched his lips move, clutching the handkerchief to her face for protection. Eventually he got up and left the room.

* * * * *

Detective Constable Graham was thoroughly exasperated. He was used to dealing with old lags. Hardened criminals with whom you could pound the desk and who would spit in your eye. The experienced ones just kept demanding a lawyer; the stupid ones tried to talk smart and would give themselves away. What he was not used to was interrogating a shrinking violet; this pale trembling reed of a woman was either Oscar-winning material or had absolutely no idea why she was there.

The Guv'nor had made it clear to him that they were on a very tight schedule for interrogating the subject. According to information received, Westwood was an accomplice of a man who was of extreme interest to the police and must be apprehended at all costs. Westwood was the last person to see him or else she was in league with him and had sent a message to a known associate on his behalf. But she didn't seem the type.

'I think she's nuts.'

The others in the observation room looked through the one-way glass at the pathetic creature clutching her handkerchief.

'No, she's not nuts. She writes chick lit.'

'Same difference, if you ask me. I'll have another shot at her.'

Graham walked down to the canteen and loaded a tray with two cups and saucers and a pot of tea. He knocked on the door before he entered the interview room – a nice touch, he thought.

'Carolanne, I've brought you some tea. My boss tells me you're a writer; I think my wife has read some of your books.'

Carolanne snapped out of her reverie. What, he had heard of her! Someone had read her books? It was very rare that anyone had ever heard of her novels. Her fear quickly subsided at the thought that she might have something of a celebrity status in this young man's eyes.

'Oh how kind, thank you. Milk and two sugars.'

'We were wondering if you could help us. We are looking for this man.'

Graham slid a photograph of Whitten across the table to her.

'Do you recognise him?'

She lifted the A5 picture and studied it intently.

'No, I can't say I do – I'm very good with faces, you know. I would have remembered if I had seen him before. What is his name?'

'He's call Seth Whitten. Does that name ring any bells?'

'No, it doesn't. What has he done?'

'We think he sent a message on your phone today. Do you know anything about that?'

There was no doubt about this piece of information. Forensics had just got back to them. They had lifted just two sets of prints from the phone: one was Westwood's and the other was Whitten's.

'A text was sent from your phone at seven o'clock this morning. Do you remember anything about that?'

'No, it couldn't have been me, or for that matter from my phone. At 7 I was walking over to the station in Great Yarmouth. I had my bag with me and the phone was in my bag. I have only sent one message today and that was on the London express, to my editors. I was supposed to meet them at 11 o'clock. I'm not going to be able to meet them, am I?'

'No, I'm afraid not, Carolanne. We need to ask you some more questions.'

'Could I possibly ring them to tell them why I won't be coming?'

'I'm afraid not, not just for the moment. I will make sure that they are informed and we will tell them that it was not your fault.'

He could see her relax. His softly-softly approach was paying off. He hoped his bosses were taking note.

'Now, can you think back – was there any time that you left your bag unattended in the station?'

As soon as the phrase was out of his mouth, he realised he was parroting the check-in girls at the airport.

'No. I walked straight through the station and onto the train. There were a lot of police around. No one could have touched my phone except me.'

'But a text was sent from your phone at 7 am. We have lifted the fingerprints of the person we are looking for from your keypad. You must have given it to him to make the call.'

'No, no!'

She was getting agitated and Graham immediately backed off.

'I didn't mean to imply anything by that, Carolanne. Perhaps I should rephrase that. We know he sent a text from your phone at exactly 7 o'clock. Please think, where were you at that precise moment?'

'I told you, I was walking across from the

Suspension Bridge to the station.'

'Sorry? You were walking from where?'

'From the suspension bridge, it's a...'

She struggled for the word. She did not want to say pub. That was low and uncouth. She did not want Detective Constable Graham to think she frequented such establishments.

'An hostelry.'

'A what?'

'An inn.'

'Oh, you mean a pub?'

'Yes, yes, as you say, a pub.'

She could feel herself blush. Not just from the shame of having been caught being so evasive but because she knew she must have sounded like a Victorian heroine from one of her novels.

'Could Whitten have interfered with your phone in the pub? Did you put it down anywhere?'

She knew at once when it had happened. There had been no one in the lounge bar, not even a barman. She thought she was safe leaving her raincoat on the chair with her phone in the pocket. How could she know some felon would rummage through her things and use her phone? She felt unclean, violated. A large tear popped out and rolled down her cheek.

'Now now, Carolanne; it's OK. It's not your fault. Just tell me what happened.'

* * * * *

'Oh bloody great! The little fucker never left Yarmouth.'

Franks was not altogether surprised. She thought it was too easy, Whitten leaving a nice fat juicy trail for her to follow all the way to London. She was getting to know this man and there was now a sneaking sense of admiration for his ability to sidestep her just when she thought she had him cornered. She would dearly love to know how he got out of the swamp undetected. Hopefully she would have the opportunity to ask him that particular question face to face.

'Get the dog teams over to the pub and start the search again from there.'

Goddamn it, they had lost nearly two hours on the wild goose chase to Cambridge! They must have only been minutes behind him and now – who knew where he might have got to.

CHAPTER 13

Seth crossed under the main road towards town and down to the tow path on the river. He had toyed with the idea of walking into town, maybe getting a taxi or a bus out of the area. Trains, he reasoned, were probably not a good idea. He was sure the police would be watching the stations. He had seen no CCTV on his trip through the hedges and billboards around the station, but trying to avoid CCTV in a built up area would be nigh on impossible. If he was to leave Yarmouth undetected, it would need to be by more unconventional means. He did not consider himself a thief, but what else could he do in the circumstances?

He had spotted a number of boats moored up near the road bridge. At this point on the river there were two public slipways for launching boats. It was not a marina, just access to the river, a good cheap place to lift any craft for service or maintenance. What he was looking for was anything that was capable of making the short sea journey, just 6 miles down the coast by his estimate, to the small fishing town of Lowestoft.

He had made this journey once before but in

the opposite direction. The family of a friend on his degree course owned a small 27ft Bayliner, moored up in a large marina on Lake Lothing in the middle of Lowestoft. His friend had a notion to make the journey up the coast to take a closer look at the Scroby Sands offshore wind farm just off the coast, a short distance north of Great Yarmouth, all part of a renewable energy project they were both working on. It had not been the happiest of experiences.

While the weather was reasonably benign, there had been perhaps a 5ft swell. The trip through the lake and out to the wind farm had been quick and without incident. The return journey was not so gentle – the wind had veered and the tide had changed, the combination generating white horses and turning the swell to chop. The boat was clearly not meant for the open sea, as he pointed out to his friend when they were finally safely back on the lake after two hours' struggling against the elements at just 5 knots: the clue was in the model of boat. It was a *Bay-liner*; if they had meant it to go offshore they would have called it an 'Out to Sea liner'. His friend was not amused.

This experience had taught Seth a number of things. First, a basic understanding of how to start a marine engine. Second, that the electronic plotters used to navigate on water were just overpriced satnavs, very similar to what you would get in a car. Third, boating was not rocket science, and fourth and most importantly, never take a Bayliner out to sea. This fourth lesson was the reason he bypassed all the shiny cruisers and speed boats as he eyed up the assembled flotilla. And there was what he was looking for, a rather scruffy 20ft wooden fishing boat with a small cabin upfront facing upstream. Large car tyres were strapped to the gunnels to act as fenders and, by the look of its stern, it had a substantial inboard diesel engine. No good for towing skiers, but more than capable of taking on a choppy sea. Just the job – now could he get it started without being caught?

He could see from the quayside that there was no door on the small 'sit up and beg' cabin, which was an immediate plus. The keys were not in the ignition, which would have been a bit much to hope for. While having a good knowledge of electronics, Seth did not want to mess with the wiring on something he was going to rely on to get him through hostile waters. He had never forgotten the old Cornish fisherman's saying: 'Them's that's not afraid of the sea – they drown; but we be afraid of the sea, and we only drown sometimes.' Not very comforting in the circumstances but a worthy lesson all the same.

He sat on the concrete steps that led down to the water and surveyed the cabin of the boat. His experience of people in general was that they were naïve when it came to security. They rarely considered the likelihood of their property being stolen or, if they did, they grossly underestimated the intelligence of the average felon. It was as he was pondering this conundrum that the air was rent by the scream of police sirens. A convoy of five cars tore across the bridge to his left. He followed the cacophony as it swept around and behind him, down into the station car park, not 50 yards away. He needed to pull his finger out. At this early hour there was no one down at the water or on the surrounding riverbanks. He stood up, walked over to the boat and got in.

The cabin was relatively clutter-free. There was a lock box – which was locked – some fishing gear and nothing else. Not many places to hide a key. Maybe he was a security-conscious guy – it had to be a guy; girls did not own scruffy fishing boats, did they? He could feel the panic rising. Where would he hide a key in such a small cabin?

A large compass nestling in the middle of the dash caught his eye. It was the standard free-floating ball type, seated in a removable plastic housing. No matter how the boat pitched or rolled, the ball with the arrow on it would always sit level and point north. The housing was marked with 360 degrees to allow for rough direction calculation and was movable to allow for adjustments over time as magnetic North continued its relentless drift eastwards, but either the captain had not made any adjustments in years or the compass was being used for more than just navigation. He levered the unit out of its housing and, to his relief, there sat a pair of keys in the pit.

He tried both keys in the lock box; the second opened it – alleluia: chocolate! For a moment his fear of capture left him and all he could think of was consuming every one of the five chocolate bars wrapped in cellophane next to the parachute flares and lifejackets. He ripped off the packaging and bit into a stale bar with gusto. With four bars gone and his hunger partially satiated, Seth returned to the more immediate task of escape. He turned the ignition key but the engine refused to fire. He turned it off and tried again.

'Come on, come on! Start, you bastard!' The beat of the struggling machine seemed deafening and he was convinced that all eyes were on him as he tried to steal the boat. He turned off the engine. He was going to flatten the batteries at this rate.

By the commotion going on at the station, Seth was sure that his exit from the swamp had not gone undetected. They had clearly tracked him to Yarmouth and he needed to get out pronto. He took a deep breath and was about to give the engine another try when he remembered the kill switch on his friend's boat. This was a little red toggle switch, which, in theory, would cut the engine if the captain left his seat unattended. Clipped to the switch was a strap, the other end of which should be Velcroed to the captain's wrist. If he tried to leave his seat, the tug of the strap would pull the switch down and kill the engine. What tended to happen in reality was that clip and strap were removed and the kill switch was used as a crude security device, left switched down when the boat was unattended to disable the engine. If anyone tried to take the boat, the engine would turn over but would not fire. Just like Seth was experiencing.

He quickly scanned around the throttle lever. There it was, level with the seat. He flicked it up and turned the key. The engine roared into life. He gunned the throttle, trying to get as much heat into the system as quickly as possible. Leaving the machine revving, Seth stepped off the boat, untied the fore and aft moorings and gave the nose of the boat a hard shove to swing it out into the river, jumping back onboard as he did so.

Passing under the old Vauxhall Bridge, he could see officers running into the station building; he was in plain sight if only they had bothered to look to their left. Within moments, the station was obscured by buildings on the bank and he was soon rounding the turn at the defunct grain elevators that brought him into Breydon Water and the 2 mile journey through the centre of town to the sea.

* * * * *

As he moved down the coast, Seth could see the promenade and all the trappings of a seaside town, the fun fairs and knick-knack shops so beloved of his childhood. He had been so focused on the shore – and staying away from it – that it had been some time since he had looked out to sea. He glanced up to the skies for any hint of a storm. There was nothing – the sky was blue and according to the navigational plotter the boat was moving over the seabed at a steady 20.5 miles an hour. He mustn't panic. In another 20 minutes Lowestoft would be in sight and he would be off the sea 10 minutes later. The coast was literally clear.

It was not long before the remains of the old gasometer hove into view. The flat landscape of East Anglia gave few markers for 'those in peril on the sea'. No headlands, no mountains to guide the way. Even Lowestoft itself didn't help – there were no church spires to be seen from the sea. In the 60s the town council had succumbed to the craze for building concrete monstrosities to house the less fortunate in society. At 15 stories, the council flats were the tallest buildings in town, but for all their height, they were still too far inland to be of any use to sailors. The gasometer would have to do; the plotter was now clearly mapping the docks and its unusual pagoda-like lighthouses.

Seth steered his craft up the broad channel and into the calm waters of the docks. The only obstacle that lay between himself and the marina was the Pier Terrace lift bridge that potentially blocked his way. Potentially because depending on the tide, he might be able to sneak under it. Apart from the fact that the operators did not want to be bothered opening the bridge for every little craft passing through Lake Lothing, this was the middle of rush-hour – or what passed for rush-hour in this neck of the woods. Lifting it would cause tailbacks and draw attention to him. He would also have to control the boat in mid-stream. What if it stalled? He scanned the walls of the pier looking for evidence of low tide. He found it – not exactly low tide, but not high tide. The boat sat a lot lower in the water than the Bayliner. He might make it.

As he closed in on the bridge, he saw the metal girders bracing the underside of each leaf. There was a slight break in the metalwork at the centre where the two sides met so he steered towards it. He knew it was going to be a tight squeeze. As the superstructure rose up to meet him, he instinctively ducked. There was a grinding noise and the boat slowed but did not stop. The twin-funnelled horn clattered into the back of the boat, rust and dust showered down onto the deck and, as he looked back, the boat's aerial could be seen hanging from the bridge. He heard a shout from above. 'You stupid ...' The rest of the admonishment was lost in the noise of the traffic and the boat's engine, but he could guess what it was. From here on in it was plain sailing.

Lake Lothing was something of a misnomer. In fact, anything less like a lake it was difficult to imagine, as over the centuries it had become Lowestoft's inner harbour. Eighty per cent of its shoreline was concrete, made up of high dock walls, rundown but still in use, and the old ship building yards with their now disused slipways and dry docks. At the far end of this monument to the worst excesses of the industrial sprawl of the early 20th century was the aptly named Haven Marina. The majority of the boats here were sea-going yachts.

At the western end of the lake, Haven faced the entrance to the beautiful Oulton Broad. Its

Boulevard Marina held barges and river cruisers that rarely, if ever, ventured east. But few of the sea-going yachts from Haven ventured west. Blocking their path were three lift/swing bridges and Mutford Lock. Less than half a mile separated the marinas of Haven and Boulevard but the boats in each were as different as chalk and cheese.

Seth was reasonably familiar with the layout of Haven, so he bypassed the first three fingers, which contained boats of up to 20m in length. He was hoping to find a spot at the far end where the smaller boats berthed. He did not want to stand out. He passed only full berths until he turned the corner of the last finger and there, halfway down a double row of yachts, he spotted an empty space.

He swung the boat in, clattering against the pontoon and juddering to a halt. With the majority of the boat now in its slot, he killed the engine and jumped onto the gangway, grabbing the painter as he did so and pulling the recalcitrant craft in tight. God, he hoped no one was looking. He took pride in being able to park Hillary in the tightest of spaces; he didn't think he would ever get the hang of parking a boat. Fortunately, the clubhouse faced the more upmarket end of the marina, so even if anyone had been looking out, they would have been unlikely to have observed his less than professional attempt at mooring.

Having tied off the boat, Seth decided to leave the keys in the ignition. He felt rather bad about this as his hope was that someone would steal it again and further muddy his tracks. He had a vague notion that if he survived, he would somehow track down the owner and compensate him for the use of his boat and the damage he had done to it.

His friend's Bayliner was just a couple of fingers away. It had everything he needed to revive him, a hot shower, clean clothes, food and drink and a dry bed. He found the keys where his friend always left them – under the cup holder in the captain's seat. The dock power was on and he flicked the switch for the hot water. After raiding the fridge for a drink, he wolfed down a couple of leftover energy bars as he hunted for jeans and a jumper. The shower, though hot, was deeply frustrating. It required sitting on the toilet with the seat down and directing the shower head where needed, all the while knocking elbows off the various protuberances that filled the tiny cubicle. It was like taking a shower in a packing case. He dried himself off with some odd-smelling towels and collapsed on the forward bunk. He had no idea where he was going but for the moment, he didn't care. A delicious stupor washed over him – he just needed to sleep.

CHAPTER 14

The dog team followed a very short scent trail. They had abandoned the search on the tracks at the station in Great Yarmouth. The pervading smell of diesel had made it impossible for the dogs to give a lead to the tracking team. Whitten had definitely not mounted the platform, of that they were sure. They knew he had dropped down onto the tracks at some point but no matter how much they widened the search circle, they could find no sign of him. The direction to the Suspension Bridge had been a godsend but the elation had been short-lived. He had entered by the back door and exited by the front, heading down to the river. Then nothing, just a row of boats. He was not on any of them.

'Sarge, it looks like he took a boat. We've asked around but no one saw him leave – they're only just waking up down here. I reckon he has a good two hours on us.'

'Damn it!' Higginbottom would have to break the bad news to Franks. He had raised expectations. They had been so close at Polkey's Mill; now he could be anywhere, up the broads or out at sea. With a heavy heart, he dialled Norwich.

'On a boat? On a fucking boat? What's with this guy? On a train, on a boat, next you're going to tell me he's on a plane and break into song. Get onto the coast guard. I want air sea rescue.'

'What will I tell them, Ma'am?'

'I don't care what you tell them. Tell them the *Titanic*'s sunk again; just get them in the air and tracking any boat that moves within a 30 mile radius of Yarmouth, no, make that 50 miles – with my luck this little shagger has picked up a cigarette boat.'

'A what, Ma'am?'

'Never mind, just get to it.'

* * * * *

Franks slammed down the phone. The optimism of the previous hour had now evaporated and she was back to square one, in fact worse than that. Whitten was no longer contained. His degrees of movement had multiplied exponentially and he was getting messages out without them being able to pinpoint his location.

'Fuck it! Spencer, get in here,' she bellowed out of her office door. 'Bring them both in, van Klaveren and the girl. They know something. If he has contacted them, maybe he has told them where he is. Make something up – whatever you like.'

'Yes, Ma'am.'

* * * * *

Franks looked through the observation room's windows at Connie and Randolph. They were handcuffed and sitting in separate locked interview rooms.

'Leave them to stew half an hour. We will focus on the girl first. She's fragile; if either of them is going to break, it will be her.'

Franks stood in the observation room looking into the two adjacent interview booths. Van Klaveren was military trained so they would probably get nothing out of him, but perhaps if they used the girl as leverage he may give something up to spare her. She decided to interview Constance herself.

Franks unlocked the door and sat down opposite her subject. Connie scowled back with a look of defiance on her face, despite her arms being cuffed behind her back, a complete change from the last time they had met. Then she thought her boyfriend was in peril and she was looking for Franks' help. This time Franks was the enemy. They both knew it.

'You're in a lot of trouble, Constance.'

Franks waited for a response. When none was forthcoming she went on.

'We know Seth has contacted you. Why didn't you tell me? Withholding information is a very serious offence – you could go to gaol.'

Not a flicker – this girl was playing hardball. Well, two could play at that game.

'I want to see a solicitor,' Connie demanded.

'And I should care because?' Franks sneered

across the table at her. 'You are under the misapprehension that I give a fuck what you want.'

Franks slowly rose from the table and walked behind the girl. They glowered at each other in the large pane of one-way glass in which their images were reflected. Suddenly, Franks grabbed a fistful of golden locks and whipped Constance's head back, at the same time ramming her knee into the back of the chair. A scream rent the air, as Connie's face was forced to point at the ceiling, causing her body to arch painfully as she tried to relieve the pressure on her neck. From the room next door, Franks could hear van Klaveren pounding on the wall. He was no doubt getting the message.

Franks stared down into Connie's shocked face and hissed, 'You're not going to need any solicitor, sister. None of this is going to court. The rules don't apply here. This is national security we are dealing with, so anything goes – get it?'

She gave an additional tug on the hair to add emphasis, eliciting another yelp from the startled girl. Franks released her hair, roughly pushing the captive's head forward as she did so. Returning to her seat, the Inspector once again questioned the girl.

'OK, so now have you anything to tell me?'

Connie glared back at her.

'Fuck off,' she spat across the table.

The girl was not going to be as much of a pushover as Franks had thought. Getting up from her chair again, she raised her right arm quickly to her head and scratched behind her ear as Connie recoiled from the expected blow. Franks laughed at her reaction then left the room, slamming the door behind her. Let her ponder on that for a while.

Franks' next port of call was van Klaveren. She had sent an officer in ahead to secure the prisoner. She was all too aware of what an Irish Ranger, retired or not, was capable of and she knew he was suitably riled.

* * * * *

At Connie's scream, Randolph had leaped out of his chair and tried to shoulder barge his way through the partition wall. This was quickly followed by the entrance of two burly constables who pulled him back down into his chair and rearranged the cuffs so they were linked through the bars in the seat back. Next time he wanted to go walkabout, he would have to take his chair with him.

It was clear this was no ordinary interrogation. Franks had crossed the line and did not mind that van Klaveren knew about it. This was a very dangerous situation in which the pair had no friends near at hand and nothing with which to bargain. Randolph needed to think quickly if he was to persuade Franks that they had no idea where Seth was. When she entered the room, he knew he was going to give her everything – it was the only way to free himself and Connie. He needed to make Franks understand that they were keeping nothing back and that to hold onto them would be pointless, if not counterproductive. Once out of custody, he could call in his markers and apply his own special skills to the situation.

Franks walked into the interview room and across to the chair, giving van Klaveren a wide berth. She was initially surprised at how calm he remained, but was soon disabused of any sense that he might be in a forgiving humour when she looked into his eyes and saw the undisguised hatred there.

'So, Mr van Klaveren, you now understand – no more games. Where is Seth Whitten?'

'If I knew, I would tell you, but I don't. He contacted Connie this morning on her mobile by text. Just a message to let her know he was still alive. That is the only contact she has had with him since he went missing. I know why you are chasing him. He has hacked e-mails and data from Norwich University and has been posting it on the net. Connie has told me this. She had nothing to do with it and tried to persuade him not to do it. This is all his idea; she knows nothing about computer hacking. You cannot hold her responsible for any of this.'

'Well, well, Mr van Klaveren. How cooperative of you. Now if only you could have been as forthcoming when we first met then there might have been no need for this unpleasantness. And then I might have believed you. But now, I'm afraid you are going to have to give me more than that. We know what he has been up to. I need to know where he is. If you don't know where he is, then you and your friend are of no use to me.' She got up to leave.

'Wait, let me talk to Connie. Perhaps she might know where he could have gone. Give me a chance.'

'OK, I'll give you half an hour. It is 11:45 – you have 'til 12:15. Don't let me down.'

* * * * *

Connie appeared at the door. Her handcuffs had been removed and she threw her arms around Randolph's neck and hugged him. The accompanying officer retreated, locking the door behind him. Randolph motioned to Connie to sit down. Without speaking he indicated to position herself so that the CCTV camera in the corner of the room could not see her face. Randolph was already sitting with his back to the camera.

Meanwhile Franks sat in the observation area watching the two of them through the one-way mirror. Their heads were down and she could not divine their expressions. Speaking in low tones, she could only catch snippets of the conversation. It was not important – the girl was going to give up Whitten or she wasn't. Either way, van Klaveren had seen the writing on the wall. He knew that if he did not come up with something, she was going to hurt the girl again. This was his weakness.

As Franks observed the pair, she heard a hesitant knock on the door. Who the hell could that be? She shouted over her shoulder, 'Yes?'

'Oh, Inspector Franks, it is Jake Tao. We spoke on the phone.'

Without turning round Franks retorted, 'What the hell are you doing here? We have nothing to discuss. Close the door on your way out.'

'Quite so, Inspector; I was just confirming my employer's message that he would no longer be needing your services.'

She saw the reflection of the silencer in the glass and dodged to one side as the first hollow point skimmed by her face. It passed through the lower edge of the mirror, blowing a fist-sized hole near the frame. As she toppled back off the chair, the second bullet caught her a glancing blow to the temple, exiting very near the entry wound and taking a large piece of skull with it.

Tao observed that it was not a clean kill. Franks lay twitching on the floor as the devastating brain trauma played havoc with her nervous system. He raised his gun again but then lowered it. Let this be a lesson to those who failed to deliver what they promised, he thought. Unscrewing the silencer from the gun barrel, he looked at the pair on the monitor, cowering behind an overturned table in the adjacent interview room. He noted the shock on their faces. He studied their features. He felt sure he would meet them again.

* * * * *

Within half a second of the bullet coming through the mirror Randolph had knocked the table over and Connie with it. They heard the second shot, which did not enter the room. He waited for 30 seconds before daring to put his head above the edge of the table. The hole in the glass had the look of a black setting sun with the cracks radiating to all corners of the mirror. Fragments of the bullet had peppered the far wall as it disintegrated on passing through the tough laminated screen.

With the chair chained to his back like some Kafkaesque beetle, Randolph shuffled on his knees to peep through the looking glass. The room was illuminated by just the light of the monitors and what little penetrated the one-way mirrors. In the dark, he could make out Franks' body, otherwise the place was empty. The sound proofing in the booth had clearly masked the sound of the silencer-suppressed gunshots and whoever had killed Franks had got clean away.

'We have to get out of here.'

'What's happened, what can you see?' Connie called out from the floor

'It's Franks. She's been shot.'

'Oh God, oh God!'

Connie started to hyperventilate. Randolph did not need this. He needed Connie fully functioning and able to help him get them both out of this dire situation. At first he had been afraid that whoever had come for Franks had come for them as well, but as the seconds ticked by his anxiety eased. Clearly the shooter or shooters had not stuck around.

Desperately scanning the room for something to get him out of the handcuffs, Randolph noticed that as the bullet had passed through the bottom of the mirror frame, it had disrupted the rubber seal that held the glass in place. If he could get Connie to put her hand through the hole, she should be able to pull the gasket out of its groove and, theoretically, the mirror should fall backwards into the observation room. He nuzzled up to Connie trying to calm her.

'Connie, Connie, listen to me. I need your help; you have to help us get out of here. Connie, look at me, look at me.'

She met his gaze with a look of sheer terror. If she continued to hyperventilate she would pass out.

'Stay with me, Connie. You need to slow your breathing. Take deep breaths. That's it, slow deep breaths.' Her panic began to ease and the mental paralysis to subside. 'Now, I need you to put your hand through the hole in the mirror and grab the rubber seal that is hanging inside. That's it. Now pull, pull hard.'

The black rubber began to detach from the frame and once it had turned the first corner, there was enough slack for Connie to pull part of it through the hole and guide it behind Randolph's back, placing it in his bound hands. Wrapping the seal tightly round his fist, he crawled across the floor, away from the mirror, dragging the ever increasing length of rubber behind him. Very quickly, the heavy glass began to split away from the frame with a satisfying cracking sound. Then suddenly, the mirror pitched backward into the observation room and fell to an angle of 45 degrees before stopping. Something on the other side was blocking it from falling to the floor. A good thing, thought Randolph, as a full forward drop would have made more noise than the gunshots.

Crawling back to the frame from his kneeling position, he gave the bottom edge of the mirror the full weight of his shoulder and it dropped the short distance to the ground with a resounding thud. Randolph held his breath – no one came. A V-shaped gap was now exposed between the glass and the frame. Plenty large enough to squeeze through provided you did not have a chair manacled to your back. Randolph needed Franks' keys and he needed Connie to get them.

'Connie, I need you to climb through the gap and get the keys off Franks' belt, can you do that for me?'

To his surprise she stood up and climbed through the gap without hesitation. A minute later, she was back with the keys, and after a few tries, she had unlocked the cuffs and Randolph had disentangled himself from the chair. His now unrestricted movement felt good. Taking Connie by the hand, he led her back through the frame and past Franks' body. He noticed that the policewoman was bleeding profusely from the massive head trauma. She was not dead but there was no surviving that sort of brain injury. He had seen men take head wounds like that. They might survive a few hours, a few days even, but death was certain to follow. He wondered who Franks' had pissed off and what it might have to do with Seth and the situation he and Connie found themselves in. He needed to talk to Seth; he needed to know how deep a shit pile he had got them into. But first of all, he needed to get them both out of the police station and as far away from Norwich as possible.

He opened the door to the observation room and took a quick glance down the corridor. There was no one between them and the double doors that led to reception. He moved them both out into the corridor and again, using Franks' keys, locked the door behind them. The longer he could delay discovery of the Inspector's body, the more time he would have to put distance between themselves and the storm that was bound to follow.

Putting his arm around Connie's shoulder, they walked slowly down to the end of the corridor where, as they approached, the double doors opened and the two officers who had bound Randolph to his chair came through. As recognition dawned, the two men raised their eyebrows in surprise but held the doors open as Randolph and Connie passed by. Randolph maintained a subdued air as they exited through the reception and out onto the street. He hailed a passing taxi and they were gone.

CHAPTER 15

Seth opened his eyes and stretched in the bunk. He felt refreshed and ready for action, but where did he go from here? Connie knew he was OK, so that problem was put to bed – for the moment. Despite the heavily financed man hunt, Seth had evaded all attempts at capture. Now pretty much home free, his next move was something of a mystery. In the meantime, he was able to access the yacht club's Wi-Fi and pulled up on his tablet the article he'd found about mining for the rare earth metals in China that Yat-sen had researched. It made for interesting reading.

Bayan-Ovoo, a Mongolian term meaning 'rich heap', is true to its name. As the regional capital of the Bayan Obo mining district of Inner Mongolia, Bayan-Ovoo has, since 2005, overseen the production of more than 45 per cent of the world's supply of rare earth metals.

This remote corner of the planet is the repository of an uncommon group of 15 minerals. No mobile phone, flat screen TV, hybrid car or wind turbine operates without them. Bayan-Ovoo had yielded this bounty to the world at a great cost to the farmers whose crops and lungs are coated each day with a toxic mix of red clay laced with uranium and thorium, a by-product of the refining process.

As Bayan-Ovoo lies in a semi-autonomous region of China, the opportunities for illegal mining and refining are legion. While many of the manufacturers of the super power-ful neodymium magnets used in wind turbines are indigenous Chinese organisations, others are foreign companies who source the rough in-gots on the black market. So long as Western companies manufacture the magnets in China, there are no export restrictions. The Chinese government imposes quotas only on countries that want to import the pure metal and its ore. This loophole means that foreign governments can guarantee their supplies of these essential elements.

Health and safety concerns do not inter-fere with the rush for riches. Local officials are paid off with sacks of cash. One ft cubed of tightly compressed renminbi bills is worth $350,000, a king's ransom to a poor factory in-spector or police chief tasked with patrolling this bandit country. Crops for hundreds of square miles around the illegal mining and re-fining sites have been failing now for years. The water sources are contaminated by the sul-phuric acid run-off from the production process.

If the mining were to stop tomorrow, it would take more than 50 years for the soil to recover – and that is never going to happen, be-cause for every top-of-the-line, direct drive, *permanent neodymium magnet generator fitted to a wind turbine, $60,000 is going into the coffers of the Chinese mob.*

The trade in rare earth metals is more profitable than drug smuggling and getting more so with every passing day. In less than 10 years, the price of a pound of dysprosium, a key element for the production of wind energy in the West, has risen 2,000 per cent. But the wealth is held very tightly by a small number of crime bosses and government officials. The Chinese government is trying to wrestle this lucrative trade from the Tong but it is too valuable to let go without a fight.

The leaking of the Climategate e-mails had got him into his current predicament, but the real story was much bigger. China was channelling funds into Norwich's Climate Centre to substantiate their exaggeration of the world's temperature. This supported the move to green energy and wind turbines specifically – which were mainly made in China. And this move to green energy increased the need for companies to buy carbon credits on the BCX and other exchanges. The Climate Centre, China, the Exchange traders and big business was making a fortune – and the taxpayer was bearing the cost. He felt he really had something with which to make the world sit up and take notice.

The news story needed to be broken and broken big; but to do that he needed help. He needed Connie. She had free movement – she could reach the journalists without being located; he could not. He needed to get a message to her without being observed.

Hard as it might be, he could not think of any solution short of returning to Norwich. This was something of a high risk strategy, but on the other hand, Norwich was probably the last place anyone would look for him. He had gone to an awful lot of trouble to get out of there so what were the chances of him coming back? But how to get there?

The train was out. He had definitely had enough of trains for one lifetime. Bus? Taxi? There was too big a risk of being spotted. For all he knew, there were now wanted posters on every tree and lamp post in the south east. He couldn't take the chance. What he needed was a car. But stealing a car these days was no easy matter. Hot wiring (even if he knew how to do it) was a thing of the past, you needed the key, but once it was reported stolen, you were easy meat. Every motorway was rotten with speed cameras; every town was peppered with CCTV. He would be picked up in no time.

He thought back to the entry into the harbour that morning. Among the myriad boat yards, one had stuck out: a wrecker's yard. It seemed odd to see a pile of old cars among all those boats. He tried to place it in relation to the marina. It had been visible shortly before he had rounded the last finger, on the same side of the lake as his berth. The cars were stacked in piles, one on top of the other like rusty skyscrapers on some post-apocalyptic New York skyline. It couldn't be more than half a mile from his current position and offered him the best opportunity for picking up a car that no one would miss.

He checked himself. Scrap yards were notorious for their physical security: the barbed wire fence, the 10ft walls topped with broken glass – the ubiquitous junk yard dog. Maybe this was not such a good idea after all. But he had seen the yard from the lake. There were no walls, no fences between the cars and the water, but the thought of trying to manoeuvre the Bayliner over to the yard filled him with despair. He needed something small and he knew just the ticket.

The Bayliner had a tiny two-man RIB with a 2 horse power outboard, ironically named *Thunder Child* after the ill-fated dreadnaught of *War of the Worlds* fame. It spent most of its life filled with rainwater, jammed under the boardwalk of the gangway, growing barnacles and sea squirts. Seth knew that the kill cord – its only form of security – was kept in a drawer. But even if he could not find it, any old piece of wire – a hair grip or a paperclip – would suffice to disable this meagre security/safety device.

Seth searched through the cabin drawers of the Bayliner for the cord without success but found a paperclip that would do the trick. Gathering his bivvy bag, computer tablet and sat. phone, he jumped onto the gangway. The RIB's engine stuck out from under the boards and, with a little levering, the rest of the rubber craft was coaxed out. Using a slime covered plastic bailer and sponge floating near the engine he soon made the tiny craft ready. To his great amusement, Seth found the kill cord still in place; the paperclip would not be needed. He loved these little four-stroke engines. They were among the simplest and most reliable mechanical devices. A bit of choke and two pulls on the starter handle and the engine buzzed into life. He sped off between the yachts and headed towards the scrap yard.

The work day was over. Seth's siesta had taken him through to 6 pm and the scrap yard was empty; the grandly named Mayfair Recycling Centre was like most businesses ringing Lake Lothing – it had a concrete quay. In a previous life it had no doubt been a boat yard. Rusty metal rungs were leaded into the flaking grey cement, making entry into the yard a piece of cake. Seth stuck his head gingerly above the level of the quay and quickly scanned for any human or canine occupation. There was none. His eye was immediately caught by a flimsy structure with plastic bags covering the window frames and an entire wall made of clear plastic sheeting. Tell-tale swathes of paint showed through from the inside. It was a spray shed. With any luck it would contain a viable automobile; who would bother spray painting a wreck?

Going in through the rickety door, his nose was immediately assailed by the pungent odour of solvents. So thick was the air that he had to open the door again to get his breath. The paint job must have been the last action of the yard's employees before finishing for the weekend. They, no doubt, had been wearing breathing masks. As he drew in a lungful of air and closed the door behind him, he felt an almighty thud, which shook the entire shack. The shock nearly floored him. He did not have to guess the origin of the impact – the guttural growls and frantic scrabbling announced the arrival of the junk yard dog.

Seth leaned his full weight against the door and peeped through the tiny glass panel at what lay on the other side. The animal was a cartoon characterisation: a Rottweiler type in a spiked collar. As the dog buffeted the door, Seth could see its saliva starting to run in rivulets towards his trainers. His lungful of air was fast running out and he needed to find a mask before the stupid mutt realised that there was only a sheet of plastic on the adjoining wall between them.

Looking through the haze of fumes, eyes streaming and lungs bursting, Seth spotted a twin-filter face mask next to the spray gun on the makeshift bench. He lunged forward, releasing the pressure on the door, which immediately gave way and the dog crashed through, its back legs slipped on the smooth concrete floor. Quickly regaining its footing, it launched itself at Seth. In a reflex action worthy of James Bond, Seth picked up the spray gun and fired. There was a loud pop. As the compressor was switched off, pulling the trigger did little more than release the last remnants of pressurised paint and solvent left in the nozzle.

However, the dog's response seemed utterly disproportionate to the feeble nature of the gun's emissions. Its attack momentarily deflected, Spike crashed into a pile of empty paint tins to Seth's left. A pitiful yelp erupted as the toxic chemicals got to work on the delicate membranes of its nose and eyes. Thrashing about blindly, the frenzied animal careered about the tiny shed like a Tasmanian Devil before plunging through the plastic sheeting and out into the yard in a headlong rush to escape the tortuous burning onslaught on its senses.

Seth piled out after the disappearing banshee, tears streaking his face. Bent double, he alternately retched and gulped in air. He collapsed in the dirt from sickness and exhaustion. If the dog had come back and chewed off his head, he could not have cared less.

After five or more minutes, Seth began to regain his composure. He slowly rose to his feet and thought about re-entering the spray shed. Looking across, he could see that between the dog and himself, they had torn down the entire wall of plastic sheeting. Together with the busted door, he was confident that the majority of the fumes would have dispersed. Gingerly sniffing the air as he approached, he could still discern paint odour.

Standing at the remains of the plastic sheet wall, he got a better idea of the vehicle that was being worked on. It looked like an early 2000 Jaguar XJ8, with green trade plates that could not be traced by the police. Perfect! The 4 litre engine produced prodigious acceleration for such a heavy car, but this was at the expense of any care for the environment.

He could not begin to imagine where the key might be kept. He opened the driver's door and to his utter amazement there it was in the ignition. Clearly the owner of the yard had a misplaced faith in Spike's guarding abilities. Half sitting into the car, Seth turned the key – nothing, not a peep out of the engine, not so much as a click. This could actually be a good thing. He pressed the electric boot release. Nothing. Radio: nothing.

In such a tight space, the car must have been driven in. He looked at the old-fashioned analogue clock in the middle of the burr walnut dash – it was six hours behind. Maybe the owner was not so overconfident about his security after all. Seth removed the key from the ignition and walked around to the rear of the car. He knew it wouldn't work but he gave the electronic boot release button a poke anyway. As he expected, there was no response.

In the low light of the shed, Seth had to look carefully to find the nondescript hole on the right-hand side of the rear number plate. Inserting the cylindrical ignition key into the hole, he twisted it to the right and the boot popped open. To his delight, he saw what he was looking for. The canny owner had detached one of the battery terminals with a ring spanner and conveniently left the spanner there for him to reattach it. Seth was rewarded with a bright flash as the two metals made contact. At the same instant, the *parp-parp-parp* of the car's horn began to blare out as the alarm circuits re-engaged. Seth jerked upward, banging his head on the boot lid and dropping the key in the wheel well as he did so. For a few seconds he scrabbled around to retrieve the key ring before silencing the alarm with the remote fob. Back in the driver's seat, he held his breath, turned the ignition key – and eight cylinders purred into life.

The next hurdle was the solid steel yard gates, which were padlocked. If he could find a big enough chain, Seth was confident the momentum of the Jag would be enough to break him out. Fortunately, junk yards are never short of chains, so after threading a heavy one through one of the loops around the gate and attaching the other end to the Jag's tow hitch, he floored the accelerator and the car lurched forward. The gate chain instantly snapped. He was free.

* * * * *

Professor Yat-sen looked out across the university campus. He would stay close to Sharkey. He did not trust any member of academia to understand the serious nature of what the Climategate e-mails had revealed. To them it was simply a threat to their job. It was pure luck and the stupidity on the part of the heads of government who were pushing the global warming agenda that a full-blown investigation into the finances behind this money-making leviathan had not been launched. Yat-sen was one of the few who knew the depth of China's involvement and the degree to which the temperature data and computer models had been manipulated to support the claim of global warming and thus necessitate green energy – and China's wind turbines in particular. They had dodged a bullet this time; next time they may not be so lucky.

Franks had made promises, promises that had not been kept. She had served her purpose in identifying Whitten as the leak, but in failing to apprehend him she had signed her own death warrant. Tao had now taken up the gauntlet. As a member of the clan, he knew what was expected of him and he also knew the price of failure. Yat-sen had also placed his own fate in these young hands; their futures were now inextricably entwined. His phone buzzed. It was Tao.

'The Inspector is dead and I have let the girlfriend and her chaperone escape from the police station. Shall I follow them to see if they make contact with the target?'

'It would please me if you were to follow them. Should they contact the target, you are to eliminate all three individuals. You have done well, Tao.'

'I understand, sir.'

'Our esteemed Master requests that no further revelations be permitted to enter the Western press. His orders are clear.'

Professor Yat-sen leaned back in his chair. Whitten had to be prevented from making any more revelations. He had to be stopped at all costs.

CHAPTER 16

As the taxi pulled away, Randolph's mind was in a whirl. What in God's name had Seth got them into? It was not at all clear what Seth could possibly have uncovered. He was investigating some sort of intrigue involving global warming. So he leaked a few e-mails he had hacked. How could that possibly warrant this sort of response? Assault in a British police station to find his whereabouts? Murder of a senior Metropolitan police officer? Who the hell could pull off a stunt like that? Who could possibly want Franks dead – apart from Randolph himself, that is?

Her manner shortly before her death had been one of confidence, not fear. She was frustrated at not being able to capture Seth, angry even, but not afraid of the consequences of a failure to apprehend. Whoever killed her must have been known to her to be able to get that close. To enter a police station carrying a gun and silencer undetected, to execute the station's most senior officer and then walk out again without being stopped – that took balls as well as brains. Whoever he was – and Randolph had no doubt it was a he, women simply did not carry out such cold-blooded killings – this guy was resourceful, cunning and utterly ruthless. A professional hit man. God help them if he turned his attentions to Connie and himself.

He drew some comfort from the thought that if the hit man had wanted them dead, he could have ended their lives at the same time as that of Franks. The perpetrator would have seen them on the monitors, seen them through the one-way glass. They were alive because he wanted them to be or maybe because he had no interest in them at all. Perhaps this had nothing to do with Seth. Could Franks have gotten on the wrong side of some underworld bigwig, who had ordered a hit on her? That was a distinct possibility; she certainly knew how to piss people off.

'Where are we going Randy?'

'We need to do a bit of dry cleaning,' he whispered.

'Come again?'

'"Dry-cleaning' it's a surveillance avoidance technique I was taught in the army. We need to pretend to do something innocuous, like going to the dry cleaners, on a pre-planned route that has surveillance traps. With any luck it actually won't be necessary. Franks is dead and her two goons let us walk out of the station unchallenged so I don't think we are being followed. But, and it's a big but, we know there are dangerous people out there, and as my mother used to say 'better to be safe than sorry'.'

'Yeh, got you, it makes sense.' Her response was a flat monotone as though she wasn't really taking in what he was saying.

Randolph's ultimate destination was an isolated farmhouse owned by another retired Irish Ranger. Ruairi McElhatton had served with Randolph in the Congo. They had seen good and bad times together. And as with any adversity, this had forged a strong bond between the two men, which neither time nor separation had diminished. Randolph knew Ruairi would take them in. He also knew that Ruairi would never betray them. The long drive up to the farmhouse would be perfect for his purposes; if Franks had had them under surveillance, which would appear to have been the case, judging from her knowledge that Seth had contacted Connie just that morning, then Randolph needed to lose any tail.

Through all his musings, Connie had remained subdued. Conversation had been minimal. To be honest, this suited him. He needed time to think. He got the taxi to drop them at a department store away from any CCTV. Mingling with the crowd, he bought two baseball caps and a couple of loose fitting light jackets. They slipped out of an emergency exit and walked down a narrow alleyway between buildings to a parallel road.

Taking Connie's bank card from her purse, he withdrew the maximum £500 from the nearest ATM. Repeating the transaction with his own card, he trousered the £1,000 and resolved not to use any further electronic devices by which they could be traced until all this was over. He had a horrible feeling that the £1,000 was going to have to last them a long time. Transactions complete, they moved away from the ATM and its CCTV camera and donned the caps and jackets. This most basic of disguises Randolph hoped would protect them from the prying eyes of passing pedestrians who might recognise them from any mug-shots that would most certainly be posted in the coming hours. Hailing another taxi, Randolph avoided making eye contact with the driver. Keeping the peak of his cap low over his face and getting straight into the back, he asked the cabby to take them to Fakenham, a small market town about 15 miles northwest of Norwich.

'Whooh, that's a long drive, mate. Are yuh sure? It'll cost yuh.'

'How much?'

'Well, if ar take it off the metre – yer not from the revenue, are yuh? Ha ha.'

The caps and the tracksuit tops were having the desired effect. They were not being taken for anyone with means.

'How much?'

'Say, 80 quid.'

'I'll give you 70 including the tip – cash.'

'Yer on.'

The very happy taxi driver set off in the direction of Fakenham. Randolph knew the fare was still a good 20 per cent above the going rate but he was buying goodwill and he always found that people were inclined to be more forgiving, and forgetful, if you had been generous.

The trip to Fakenham was part of the dry

cleaning. The long flat single carriageway A1067 gave ample opportunity to monitor following traffic.

'Where 'bouts in Fakenham de ye and the young lady want droppin', then?'

'Town centre will do fine.'

'Right y'are, mate.'

Randolph was distracted; he was half leaning against the back door, which allowed him to view the traffic behind them without too obviously looking out of the back window. It was Friday afternoon and the weekend exodus from the city had begun. The road was busy and it was hard to discern which, if any, of the following vehicles were engaged in any sort of pursuit.

The driver had four children, one of whom was about to begin studies at Norwich University.

'Studyin' emviroment, she is. Clever girl, our Lucy.'

Randolph maintained polite conversation for the 40-minute journey. During this time Connie said not a word.

'Young lady. She OK?'

'Bad traveller, I'm afraid.'

'Does she want to sit up front?'

'No, thanks. She'll be OK if she keeps her eyes closed.'

'Poor dear.'

Drawing into the town, Randolph removed four notes from his wallet, handing them over to the driver as he pulled up outside a hotel.

'This do yuh?'

'Yeah, fine.'

He and Connie got out and walked away down the street, stopping for a moment to look in a shop window. Within minutes the taxi had picked up another fare. The two retraced their steps and walked through an archway and into the small courtyard of the Crown Hotel. Sitting down at a round table set out on the cobbles, Randolph ordered a pot of tea for two and turned his attention to Connie. She hadn't spoken in over an hour and he was beginning to get worried.

'Drink your tea – it will help.'

She clasped both hands around the hot cup and sipped the strong sweet brew.

'Franks is dead, isn't she?' Connie's need for Randolph to repeat his earlier assertion did not surprise him.

'Yes.'

As she returned the cup to the saucer the two rattled together and Connie tried to stabilise them.

'Will they come after us as well?'

'I don't know; I don't know who "they" are.'

'What are we going to do, Randy?'

Her voice was surprisingly calm. She hadn't dissolved in a flood of tears, which had been his biggest fear. He did not want to draw attention from this moment on. He wanted to break any connection there might be between Randolph van Klaveren and the city of Norwich. There was no point in dry cleaning if you made a scene at some future location that meant you could be re-acquired.

'I have a friend, an old soldier who owes me one. He will take us in. No one will find us. He is a couple of hours away, a few more taxi rides – we can't risk hiring a car. We need to stay below the radar. The police are going to want to talk to us about Franks so we can't go back to Norwich until we know what is going on *and who killed her*. Contacting anyone may put them in danger too. We need to talk to Seth and find out what he knows.'

* * * * *

Seth was doing his level best to stick to the 30 mile per hour speed limit through the town. This was painful – it seemed as though he could walk faster. The subdued road noise and muffled engine sound gave him the sensation of being in a cocoon. For an old girl, the Jag rode as smooth as you like.

Norwich was less than an hour's drive, even in Friday evening traffic. He flicked on the radio which promptly asked him for a security code. Of course, the battery had been disconnected. Looking around, Seth found the 4 digit number on a yellow Post-it in the ashtray. How convenient. With the radio up and running, he tuned to a news channel and was intrigued by the breaking news story. An inspector Jean Franks of the Metropolitan Police Force had been murdered at the Wymondham headquarters of the Norfolk constabulary. The intrigue quickly turned to horror.

'Three individuals are being sought by police

in connection with the killing. A Chinese national known as Jake Tao, thought to be an alias, an Irish national, Randolph van Klaveren, and a UK citizen, Constance Bennett.'

'Holy crap!'

Seth hit the brakes and pulled the car onto the verge. His sudden manoeuvre generated much blaring of horns and gesticulations from his fellow road users, to which he was totally oblivious. Turning up the radio, he sat open mouthed as the details of the murder spilled out over the airwaves. Connie involved in murder with two guys he had never heard of? Wait a minute, Randolph van Klaveren. Yes, he remembered now – an Irishman from Dublin. Connie had mentioned him once. He'd always thought van Klaveren was a crazy name for an Irishman. But what was he doing over here with Connie and what had either of them to do with this Chinaman? Jesus Christ. There was no point in going to Norwich. They must be on the run – join the club.

His mind was in turmoil. The thought of the Chinaman sent a sudden shiver down his spine. This could be no coincidence. All his troubles started when he began leaking details about Yatsen. If Yat-sen was in some way linked to the Tong, then he had brought down the most terrible curse on all their houses. If they were working with this Tao fellow, then all three of them were in terrible danger. He needed to warn them, if it was not already too late.

* * * * *

After the third taxi ride, Randolph and Connie were nearing their destination. Randolph was confident that he had done all that was necessary to lose any possible tail. All the same, he was taking no chances. The last drop off was at a bus stop on a lonely road in Harlow Wood, about 3 miles outside Mansfield in Nottinghamshire, the heart of rural England. In days of yore, this had been Robin Hood country. At this moment Randolph felt a certain kinship with the mythical outlaw.

'Are you sure this is the spot? There might not be another bus along here this evening.'

'No, this will be fine.'

'If you're sure.'

Money changed hands and the taxi made a U-turn before speeding back in the direction of Nottingham. Connie and Randolph were both beat and hungry to boot but there was some foot slogging to be done before they could rest. Once the taxi was out of sight, the two headed towards the crossroads through which they had just passed. This was the last bit of the dry cleaning, real belt and braces, probably unnecessary but he was taking no chances. At the junction, Randolph paused. The roads were clear in all directions. There was no suspicious van with blacked out windows parked at the roadside, no helicopters hovering overhead. He was sure they had not been followed. Taking a left, they began walking down Rickets Lane. After a few minutes, Connie piped up.

'Are we there yet?'

They both laughed. It was good to see a smile on her face again. Had it only been that morning that their joy at the knowledge that Seth was still alive had turned into the despair in which they now found themselves?

'I'd say we've about a mile to go. It's been over 20 years since I was last around these parts.' He was having difficulty losing the frontier theme.

'Are you sure he still lives here – how do you know we will be welcome?'

'Still exchange Christmas cards, and as for whether we will be welcome, I don't know about me but I know you will be. Ruairi always had an eye for the ladies.'

Connie blushed. It didn't take much; any sort of innuendo was likely to make her cheeks glow.

'No, seriously. I mean, does he have a wife, partner or whatever?'

'Yes, Cheryl. I think you'll like her. She is the reason he left the Emerald Isle; must have been love.'

They walked on in silence, finally stopping at a large white farm gate barring the entrance to a long, deeply rutted track leading to a farmhouse 500 yards in the distance. The gate was securely locked, though this was of no consequence to the postman who had stuffed the gate-mounted post box with the usual mixture of junk mail and bills. Pulling out all the protruding paper and any that he could fish out with two fingers, Randolph folded them into his pocket and helped Connie climb over.

'Do you think they have a guard dog?'

'More than likely, but I doubt it could be too vicious. The fences and hedges around here don't look that secure so they could hardly have a Doberman patrolling the grounds. Probably makes a lot of noise but keeps its teeth to itself.'

As if on cue, barking started up from the direction of the house, quickly followed by admonishments from a female voice.

'Quiet, Sabre, shut up, will you?'

As they rounded the corner of the hedge lining the driveway, they encountered a slender woman in her sixties bending over a large black mutt of dubious parentage. She looked up sharply as she heard them approach.

'Who the hell are you?'

'Ah Jesus, Cheryl have I aged that much?'

The scowl fell from her face and she ran over with open arms, grabbing Randolph around the neck and hugging him closely to her.

'Randy, this is wonderful! What a surprise. In God's name, what are you doing here?'

Reaching into his pocket, he exclaimed, 'I've brought you your post.'

'Away with you, you old tease. And what's with the caps? You look like a couple of chavs. Now tell me, who is this fine lass?'

'This is Connie, daughter of a close friend. I'm charged with looking after her but of late I've not been doing a very good job. That's why we're here. We need a place to stay, to lay low for a few days. The caps are our disguises.'

'Not much of one, if you ask me.'

'Well, they fooled you, didn't they?'

She laughed. 'Come inside, you look wrecked,' she said, leading them into the house. 'Ruairi will be back soon. He's just popped into the village for groceries. What can I get you?'

'I could murder a bacon sarnie.'

'How about you, dear?'

'I really need to use the bathroom.'

'Sure thing. Through the door second on your right. The door sticks a bit; you need to give it a shove.'

When Connie had left the room, Cheryl's face took on a more serious look.

'What's wrong, Randy? Why all the cloak and dagger stuff?'

'Not to put too fine a point on it, Cheryl, we are in the shit, shit up to our armpits. Have you seen the evening news?'

'You're kidding me, aren't you? You're not on the evening news?'

'I don't know. Put it on and let's see.'

She picked up the remote and the screen sprang into life.

'...and at the top of the hour, Metropolitan murder. Tonight's top story. A senior inspector in the Metropolitan Police Force has been found shot dead at the headquarters of the Norfolk Constabulary. Police are hunting two men and one woman in connection with the murder. One of the men is Asian and has been named as Jake Tao. The other man is Irish. The woman is English. A terrorist link has not been ruled out. For further details we cross over to our East An-

glia correspondent…'

Cheryl killed the sound as Connie re-entered the room. All three stared at the screen. Behind the reporter were clear mug shots of Randolph and Connie and a grainy CCTV still of a Chinese- looking man tagged as Jake Tao. As they stood there in mute amazement, Cheryl finally broke the silence.

'Who's your Chinese friend?'

'I have absolutely no idea, but what I can tell you is that he is the shooter.'

'You haven't brought him here have you, Randy?' He could see real fear in Cheryl's eyes.

'No one followed us. I am absolutely certain. We even came the last mile on foot. We didn't do that for the good of our health.'

'Ruairi's out of all that stuff now, you know that, don't you? I couldn't bear to go back to not knowing. You were in the thick of it; I think you even enjoyed it. I was stuck here; it was torture. I don't ever want to experience that again.'

'Heh, what's all the shouting about?'

A tall weather beaten man of indeterminate age stuck his head around the door and gave a big smile to everyone, a smile that grew in intensity as his gaze fell on Randolph and recognition dawned.

'Randy, you old son of an Irish whore, I hear you're in a bit of a bother. Who have you been shooting up this time, you old terrorist? You're all over the news. Let's have a drink. Get the man a drink, Cheryl; it's not every day an Irishman gets to shoot some Brit police officer and lives to tell the tale.'

'Be serious, Ruairi, this is tragic. A woman has died and Randy did not shoot her.'

Ignoring his wife, Ruairi strode up to Randolph and gave him a bear hug.

'Great to see you, old man; have a whiskey – you look as though you could use it. And, the little lady, what will you have?'

'I'll have a brandy, if you have any.'

'Good woman yourself! Now we haven't been properly introduced. As you have probably guessed, my name is Ruairi and from your gorgeous picture on the telly you must be Constance.'

'Connie. Please call me Connie.'

He smiled affectionately as he handed her a large brandy glass and she immediately took a heart-warming slug. As it hit her stomach she could feel the effects start to sooth her jagged nerves. Boy, she needed this.

'So Randy, what's the story?'

* * * * *

'Do you think they have reached their final destination, Tao?'

'I believe so. Their exact location is unknown to me. However, the surrounding road network would lead us to believe that they are within a 1 mile radius of their last observed position. His behaviour during the past four hours clearly shows that the man has sophisticated knowledge of anti-pursuit techniques. His name is Randolph van

Klaveren. He has a military background but our sources tell us that he is no longer active.'

'This gives me cause for concern, Tao. You say he is not under observation.'

'This is so; his last manoeuvre made it impossible for the pursuit vehicles to maintain contact without revealing to him the nature of their task. He cannot leave the area without being observed. There are only five dwellings within the search perimeter. We estimate that his exact location will be established within 12 hours.'

'Report to me when you have re-established contact. Ensure that the pursuit team do not expose their presence. The two individuals are not the primary target; they are, however, our only link to the primary target. Maintain full electronic surveillance. It is imperative that they do not get away.'

CHAPTER 17

In the farmhouse kitchen Cheryl and Ruairi sat open-mouthed as the fugitives related their story. The behaviour of Inspector Franks had them both apoplectic with indignation that a serving member of Her Majesty's Constabulary could employ such crude bully boy tactics on one so young. The subsequent detail of her sudden and violent demise did not elicit the same degree of outrage that it might have done under different circumstances.

'Go to the police. Tell them what happened; tell them what a bastard Franks was. Surely they will believe you.'

'Maybe, Cheryl, but what if they don't? What if this conspiracy, or whatever the hell it is, goes deeper than we know? The police might simply hand us over to whoever is behind this and that's the last you'll see of us.'

'No, Randy, that can't be so.'

'Look, most of the world's policing doesn't operate by the rules of fair play, tea and cucumber sandwiches. Come on; back me up here, Ruairi. You've been there, you know how it works.'

Randolph was getting irritated by Cheryl's naïve, simplistic view of law and order.

'Randy's right pet. It could be suicidal to hand yourself in without knowing who you are dealing with and who you can trust.'

'OK, then what next? Are you going to spend the rest of your lives holed up in this place? I don't think so.' Cheryl was getting angry.

'Not in these shoes.' Connie's attempt at humour went down like a lead balloon.

'So you think this is funny, do you, missy? Isn't it your boyfriend who has got us all into this predicament? Heaven preserve us, we could all wake up dead in our beds.' Cheryl turned on her heel and stormed out of the room.

'Go after her, Ruairi. She's right to be angry.' The two men exchanged pained glances as the big Irishman went to mollify his wife.

'I can see why you failed the entrance exam to the diplomatic core.' Randolph gave Connie a wan smile.

'Sorry, I don't know what I was thinking. I was trying to make things better. I just made them worse.'

'Too true, though she'll get over it. Fear does that to people. She has a big heart, does Cheryl, but we mustn't let emotion get in the way of coming up with a solution that does not involve going to the police.'

'I've been wracking my brains about how to get in contact with Seth. I'm sure he is thinking the same thing. It was clear from Franks' frustration that the police have no idea where he is; otherwise they would not have taken the drastic measures they did. If it had not been for the crazy Chinaman, we would still be in her clutches and I'm not sure which of the two would be worse.' Connie's brow was furrowed in thought.

'We need to talk to Seth. He can tell us if there is any link between Franks' death and what he has been working on, or whether it was just some horrible coincidence and Franks had simply annoyed one gangster too many.'

'I feel that if Seth was to use any method to reach me, it would be through the Internet. It's what he knows best.'

'How would he do that?'

'I don't know – email, Facebook, a website maybe? He could put up a website that only I might find and leave a message for me there.'

'Yes, but how would you know what to look for? Bit of a long shot, don't you think?'

'Look, I'm just brainstorming, all right? If you shoot down every idea I come up with, we'll get nowhere.' Connie was getting impatient.

'Sorry, you're right, go on. What about email?'

'Well, he could send an encrypted email to one of my accounts. The only problem with that is I'm sure the police will be monitoring my messages, and while it will not give away our position, it would certainly give away his. It needs to be a message that only I can understand, like "gamma ray bursts", but rather than just letting me know he's alive, it must allow a two-way conversation that would only make sense to us.'

'So how would he do that?'

'I tell you what, Facebook would work. He could leave messages on my wall, even pictures. Done the right way, no one would guess it was him. I could just be chatting to one of my friends.'

'Oh yeah, on the run from the police, accused of murder, "just thought I'd ask you what you thought of the latest JLo movie"?'

'OK, maybe not chatting but I'm sure some of my girlfriends have tried to contact me on Facebook after they've seen the news. It's what friends do.'

'Do you think you will have any friends after this? After all, who wants a convict as a mate?'

'Ha ha, just ask Ruairi if they have the Internet in this godforsaken place. I'm not hopeful by the low-tech look of this kitchen. I'm surprised they have a television.'

'Don't let Cheryl hear you say that. You're in her bad books as it is.'

'Don't let me hear what?' Cheryl walked back into the kitchen looking a little less hostile.

'We were just wondering if the Internet had reached this far into the backwoods.'

'Watch yourself, Randy, or you'll be sleeping outside with the dog. I'll have you know we've just been upgraded to an 8-megabyte link.'

'Don't you mean megabit?' chirped Connie. 'Eight megabytes would be 64 megabits and unless you're running fibre, I doubt you're getting that speed.'

'Watch it, honey; you're so sharp you just

might cut yourself. Megabits, megabytes, could be squashed strawberries and rubber bands, for all I care. All I know is it lets me Skype the kids in Australia and I get to see my grandchildren. The laptop's in the drawing room; don't break it now, child.'

Cheryl was obviously feeling needled. Randolph was definitely going to have to get Connie to back off if they were to live in peace and harmony for however long their stay lasted.

'Connie's just going to check her Facebook page.'

'Now that's what I call a child of the noughties. Death and destruction all around, but she must check her Facebook page.' Cheryl looked exasperated.

'It's not like that; she is hoping to get a message from her boyfriend, the one who "got us all into this predicament", as you so gently put it. He's a smart kid by all accounts and we need to know what he knows, especially in relation to this Chinese guy.'

'Oh my God!'

They rushed into the lounge where Connie's contorted face was staring at the laptop.

'What is it? Has he left a message?'

'No, it's Tony. There's a message from Tony – some sick bastard has put up a message pretending it's Tony Marshall.'

'Who's Tony Marshall when he's at home?'

'He was an ex-boyfriend from undergrad days.'

'OK, so why the drama?'

'When we graduated, I went on to do a Masters; he went off to become a pilot. His aircraft ditched in the Irish Sea on a training flight. They never found his body.'

'Could it be him?'

'No, no. The message is all chatty, no mention of the crash. It's just some sicko playing a joke. I'm just a bit upset, that's all.'

'As a matter of interest, what does he say?'

'What are you talking about? Who cares what he said.'

'Come on, Connie, you're a clever girl. What's the likelihood that someone would go to the trouble of hacking into the Facebook account of a dead person just to send you a chatty note for a bit of a laugh? You're a girl on the run. Any mention of your murder charge?'

'You're right. It's like he hasn't seen the news.'

'Now just calm down a bit and read the message again.'

Hi there, a raise from the grave, eh? Over in New York last week, visited that restaurant again we ate at with your family last year. The meal was deadly.'

'Well, Tony never met my family last year or any other time. He was a bit "wrong side of the tracks", if you know what I mean; never got serious enough for meeting the parents kind of thing.'

'Your love life is all very interesting, but is this Seth?' Now Randolph was getting impatient.

'Yes, for sure. He did meet my parents – much more presentable! We had a fantastic meal at this really expensive Chinese restaurant called Tao… He is clearly warning us off the Chinese assassin. Well, duh, tell us something we didn't know, smarty pants.'

'It's not so stupid. Think of it from his perspective. It looks like we were broken out of a police cell by Tao, so we could have been working with him. The police certainly think so. How was Seth to know any different? When did he send the message?'

'Only 50 minutes ago. He might be still online. Quick, what should I say?'

'Let me think, let me think. Cheryl, any thoughts? You're good at the idle chit-chat?'

'Watch yourself, Randy. Well let me see. In my experience, innuendo is always good for getting across a difficult message without spelling out what it really is.'

'How do you mean?'

'Well, if you wanted sex for instance and you were too coy to ask.'

Connie's face glowed red, right on cue.

'Aren't we a delicate little flower, then?'

'Come on, Cheryl, stick to the task and stop baiting the girl.'

'As I was saying, if you were too coy to ask, you might say something like "Let's play hide Mr Wibbly Wobbly policeman's helmet."'

'Very funny but how does that help us?'

'Look, I'm sure this young couple haven't remained utterly chaste these last few years. They must have some pillow talk or bedroom language that might be useful within which to hide a message that only they would understand.'

'Augh, God no, that would be just too embarrassing.'

'You mean even more embarrassing than "gamma ray bursts"?! She's right, Connie. You need to come up with something so he will know it is you talking and not Tao and you need to do it quickly while he's still there.'

'Give me a moment. OK, OK.'

She typed: *'Hi Shit Pot. As I recall the food at that restaurant was crap. I wouldn't go there again lol.'*

'"Shit Pot"? You have to be kidding me. Who calls their lover Shit Pot?' Ruairi had entered the room and was enjoying the banter immensely.

'Look, I can't do this if you are going to ridicule me.'

'Yes, everyone give the girl a chance. I thought that was pretty good. I am sure he will have got the message that we know Tao is dangerous. Now, while we wait for a reply, we need to decide what we want to ask him and what we want to tell him.'

'How about telling him where we are and we could arrange to meet and plan our next move, face to face. I really miss him, you know?'

'Sympathetic as I am to your need to get back together again, until we know how secure both our locations are, I think it would be a mistake to risk a rendezvous.'

'I'm with Randy on this one. He and I worked some difficult terrain together and one of the things we learned is that you never knew who was watching or who might be following you. I know you were super careful getting here but better to err on the side of caution. Kept us alive all these years, eh mate?'

With that, Ruairi gave Randy a hefty slap on the back. Connie refreshed the page and a new message was already in.

'Fantastic, he's still there. He says "Ah the food wasn't that bad, what was really dangerous was kissing with tongues in front of your parents" – what does that mean? Dangerous, it would have proved fatal if he had tried that in front of my mother. That never happened.' A look passed between Randy and Ruairi.

'What, what does he mean? You know, don't you?'

'Are you thinking what I'm thinking, Ruairi?'

'He's Tong.'

'What does that mean? Will you stop all this cryptic stuff and tell me.'

Connie glared at the two men. She could tell by the looks on their faces that she was not going to like the answer.

'Jake Tao. Seth thinks he's from the Chinese mafia. They're called the Tong. Tongue – tong, get it?'

'Is that bad?'

'"Fraid so. Italy: 60 million population; China: 20 times the size. Think Camorra on steroids. These are not nice people. Seth must have good reason for thinking this; otherwise he would not have worried us.'

'Well, what can we do?'

'About the Tong? Best we can do is just keep away from them. Your good buddy has stirred up a hornet's nest if the Tong are interested in him. How do you think he did that?'

'The only Chinese link is the one I told you about in Norwich, Randy, when Seth asked me to look through the e-mails he had decrypted between Professor Sharkey and Professor Jiang Yat-sen. But Yat-sen is based at Stanford University in American; he isn't in China.'

'No, but he travelled to China regularly to gather temperature records. I read about him on the Internet recently. He got himself into trouble with the university's ethics committee. They were investigating him for misuse of grant aid – the data he was providing had been fixed. If Seth is saying that Yat-sen is also a member of the Tong, then the Tong for some reason are interested in making the global warming problem look as bad as possible. Seth must have made the link and the Tong don't want him breaking the news. Hell's bells, that's why Tao didn't kill us when he had the chance, he needs us to get to Seth. Oh shit.' Now it was Randolph's turn to worry.

'But we're safe, right? They don't know we're here. Please tell me we lost them.'

'There's no way of knowing. I can be sure as I am of anything that they don't know we are in this farmhouse but if they're good, if they're very good, they could know we are in the area and, with the resources they have at their disposal, I imagine it would not take them too long to narrow down the search. I think we are safe for the moment. They are not going to approach us so long as they think we can lead them to Seth. Once they know we are on to them, then our goose is cooked.'

The two women did not take the news well. The matter-of-fact way that Ruairi and Randolph laid out the doomsday scenario gave the whole exchange a surreal air. How could this be happening? This was rural England, not downtown Macao.

'Now we have got to stay calm. We've got out of worse scrapes than this, eh Randy?'

'Say, Ruairi, what about the press? If the TV or a major newspaper showed interest in the story, maybe that would scare off the Tong. They are notoriously media shy. If we could get the BBC or somebody to break the story, put the record straight and clear our names, then perhaps the police could put us into protective custody while they hunt down Tao, or at least until they are sure he has left the country.'

'Sounds like a plan.'

Connie once again brought the conversation back to Seth. 'But don't we need more information from Seth? We need to know what the Tong's interest is in all of this. He made the link first. We need to know what it is and get that out into the public arena. Once we have done that, then neither Seth nor us are of any interest. Apart from revenge; in fact it would go very badly on a political level if anything were to happen to us. A Chinese national killing a senior British police officer is bad enough; surely they would not want to make things worse by allowing us to be killed.'

'I like your reasoning, Connie. This could be our way out, but as you say, we need to know what links the global warming agenda with the Tong. Anything else from Seth?'

'No, but then we haven't replied to his last message. We need to ask the question, but how to do it without alerting Tao?'

'You're right; we have to assume that he is monitoring this conversation. Let's hope he hasn't twigged what's going on.'

* * * * *

'It would have been better, Tao, if your involvement in the death of Franks had been less obvious.'

Yat-sen had felt obliged to contact the specialist without waiting for his report back on the whereabouts of van Klaveren and the girl. His worst fear that Tao would not be able to handle the subtleties of the situation had been realised.

'My contacts in the US administration inform me that the American secret service have become interested in the death of the policewoman. This will not go down well with our brothers in Shanghai. It was a grave error for you to allow your name and picture to become available to the news media.'

'A thousand apologies, sir; it will be my task to redeem my honour. I have good news; the location of the pair has been established once again. One of the five dwellings we had identified belongs to a retired Irish Ranger, a Ruairi McElhatton. He served with van Klaveren. In view of the unanticipated interest of the Americans, how should I proceed?'

'Has Whitten made any attempt to contact the girl?'

'No. There has been no telephone communication of any kind in or out of the house. There is low level Internet traffic but no e-mails or data exchange.'

'For the moment remain unobserved. It is my belief that Whitten will try to contact the girl very soon. Hold station; inform me if there are any developments.'

* * * * *

'What the hell are you doing these days? Last I heard you were shagging some floozy from Stanford. How'd you get on with her?'

Seth sat in an internet café in Nottingham reading Connie's cryptic message. She wanted to know about Yat-sen, his connection to the Tong. He wondered how he could explain the mining of rare earths, underworld involvement and the manufacture of wind turbines. Seth bounced back a reply. *'It's all very complicated; you know what girls are like. Anyway, what's it to you? It's not as though we're going out anymore?'*

'Don't be so coy; are you afraid I'll blab your dirty little secrets all over the news? Maybe that wouldn't be such a bad idea – put some manners on you, it would.'

So, he mused, Connie wanted to go public, but he couldn't do it with just his half of the story and she couldn't do it with just her half. They needed to put the whole thing together. The murder of Franks gave them just the level of drama that they needed to expose the corruption surrounding global warming, but he didn't know what happened when Franks was killed.

He was beginning to get frustrated. He was worried that Connie had pushed things a little too far by mentioning Stanford, but with any luck, if someone was reading this drivel, their mind would already have turned to mush and they would miss any hard clues. He was finding it difficult enough to make sense of it himself. Someone needed to tell their story. His side of it was all about money trails, rare earth mining, pollution and corrupt scientists. Their story was about murder, intrigue, organised crime, vindication and a pretty girl. There was no contest; the story that the public would latch onto was obvious. Connie needed to tell her story and piggyback the global warming angle.

He had decided what must be done. It was getting late and he could see that the owner of the internet café was anxious to close up.

'Do you sell memory sticks?'

'Yes, sir, 1 GB, 2 GB, 4 GB, 8 GB sticks.'

'I'll take two 1 GB sticks, thanks – just need to download some stuff.'

The man looked pleased with his extra revenue; it had been a slow day. Seth spent 15 minutes downloading relevant web information and creating a Word document on which he told the story and made the links. Putting everything into one folder he dumped a copy onto each stick. He then sent his parting message to Connie.

'Got to go now, Sweetpie. Keep the fairy pocket warm for Mr Tumnus.'

He knew his signing off would upset her – and, if anyone was there, deeply embarrass her – but he needed to set the scene for the following day. She would not understand what he was saying, but hopefully tomorrow that would change.

* * * * *

'Why isn't he responding?'

'Maybe he's thinking; I hope he can come up with some idea of getting us his information on the Tong. If we are to go to the press, we will need the whole story. We are only going to get one shot at this. Has anyone had any thoughts about who we should approach?'

'Ruairi's right, I think we need to go to the BBC. There's a guy that Seth was impressed with; he's some sort of weather and climate expert. Unlike most at that august body, this bloke seemed to take a very even-handed look at the subject. I've forgotten his name but I will remember it when I see it. Give me a moment.'

211

Connie's fingers whirred over the keys as she made a quick search of BBC correspondents.

'That's the fellow, Anthony Thoroughgood. Ex-UK Met Office, knows the subject from the ground up. He might be a bit loath to stick his head above the parapet with just the global warming part of our story but he is not going to be able to resist the murder angle.'

'Knowing who to send this stuff to is the easy bit; getting it to him, now that's going to be some neat trick. We have to assume that at all times we are under surveillance, both electronically and physically.' Ruairi was always the pragmatic one.

'Oh dear God, I'm not going to be able to sleep tonight.'

'Look, Cheryl, if they had wanted us dead, we'd be dead by now. Our value to them requires us to be alive and act as a lure to bring Seth to them. Whatever we do, they must not be given Seth's location. He has studiously avoided saying or even hinting at where he is. Equally, we cannot let him know where we are lest he decides to take a risk and come here.'

'Wait, hold it everyone, he's back. Oh no! He says he's leaving.'

Even the overtly sexual nature of the message did not raise a blush on Connie's cheeks. Her despair was palpable. No one made any jokes; there was silence.

'What the hell's he playing at? We were talking. It was working. Why did he have to go and leave?' Connie looked bereft.

Randolph tried to mollify her. 'Chin up, pet. I'm sure he knows what he's doing. We need to monitor the connection 24/7. Let's do this in relays, two hours on, six hours off. No one gets too bored or too tired.'

'I'll take the first stint. I can't believe that he has gone off and left me. Perhaps the threat of someone listening in has made him so cautious that he is leaving false messages to put them off the scent.'

'OK, Connie, but I think Ruairi should take the next two hours so you can both sleep through the core hours. You look as though you need it. I'll clear out the two spare rooms; they've accumulated a lot of junk since the boys left home.'

The three of them trooped out of the lounge and left Connie to her thoughts.

'How's she holding up, Randy?' Cheryl looked concerned.

'The incident in the police station shocked her, but she's come round. Turned out to be tougher than I thought; from a sheltered upbringing to being assaulted, shot at and seeing someone with their brains all over the carpet is probably enough to send anyone over the edge. Re-establishing contact with Seth, even in this stilted manner, has given her a new lease of life. So for now, I think our next objective, 'til we get the other half of the story from Seth, should be to think of a way of contacting this BBC hack without Tao finding out.'

'I think sometimes we get so wrapped up in

email and text and Twitter that we forget snail mail. I write to the boys in Oz. A letter can take five days to get to them but if we catch the right collection, in this case, we could have the details of the story to the BBC within 24 hours.'

'That's a fine idea and to think, I thought I'd married a bimbo.' Ruairi's remark provoked a well-deserved clip round the ear from Cheryl.

'Randy, how about getting something down on paper, a basic outline of the way you think things have developed? Your side of the story regarding the policewoman's murder, Connie's torture and how Seth's hacking of the e-mails seemed to trigger all these events. Out him as "Deep Cool", he'll love that.'

'I'll get onto it.'

* * * * *

Details of the Google search were recorded and the bio of the BBC correspondent was relayed to Tao. Without hesitation, Tao contacted an asset in London.

'You have the details of the man? I require confirmation of his location within one hour.'

Tao was under no illusion as to his predicament. His sloppy work in Norfolk had brought attention to the Tong; he was ashamed. He would now do everything in his power to redeem his reputation. In under an hour, Anthony Thoroughgood was being followed; his life expectancy was now measured in days. This time there would be no cameras; nothing to link his death to the Tong.

Yat-sen lifted the receiver. 'Yes Tao?'

'The farmhouse has made an Internet search on an Anthony Thoroughgood, a BBC environmental reporter. It is my belief that they will soon try to make contact. We have him under surveillance. How shall I proceed?'

'This news concerns me greatly. Has there been any contact between the farmhouse and Whitten?'

'None that we can discern.'

'It may be that they wish to reveal what transpired in the police station. This must not be allowed to take place. If they make any attempt to send a message to this man, kill him. Make it look like an accident.'

Tao smiled – this was more his line of work.

PART IV

To kill an error is as good a service as, and sometimes even better than, the establishing of a new truth or fact.

Charles Darwin

This had to be the easiest way to make money that had ever been invented. As Robin Borrington stood gazing on the frenetic activity that was the floor of the BCX, he could not believe his luck. At 25, he was one of the top performing traders on the Exchange. He had always been interested in making a fast buck. Not a slow buck or even a buck travelling at moderate speed, no, a fast buck. After completing a fun degree in History and Politics at Georgia Tech, he had tried his hand at a number of endeavours ranging from second-hand car sales to peach farming. All had ended badly, especially for his creditors. But carbon trading, this was more like it.

It had all begun when he read an online ad: 'Carbon Credit Investments – Are you interested in trading Carbon Credits for 300 per cent+ returns?' You bet he was! Most able-minded individuals would have had a quiet chuckle to themselves and moved on, but Robin believed that these returns were possible and this had resulted in a very profitable association with Clean Sky Capital. He quickly learnt that this new market had grown from just $8.3 million in 2005 to over $125 billion in 2009, a truly awe-inspiring expansion of over 3,000 per cent per annum – during a period when the rest of the world's economies had declined – what was the catch? None that he could see.

Clean Sky Capital operated in both the United States and Europe, trading carbon credits on the BCX and the European Climate Exchange, the ECX. Soon Australia and Japan would be opening their own trading floors and it was this that Borrington saw would make him the billionaire he had always dreamed of. Simon Traynor was Robin's God. He headed up the BCX and quickly became the darling of the Green movement. By 2007 he was being hailed by

Time Magazine as a 'Hero of the Environment'. But it was what Traynor was projecting for the future of carbon trading that had really excited Borrington. A $10 trillion worldwide carbon market, a further 80-fold increase in the market size – and little old Robin was in there on the ground floor, perfectly positioned to cash in on this tsunami of an opportunity. If only his maths teacher could see him now.

He quickly got the hang of the simple trade flips that were making him so wealthy. It was not too different from buying and selling second-hand cars really. Buy low, sell high, how difficult could it be? On any particular day Robin might buy a million carbon credits from Acme Wind Farm Inc., USA, at $20 per tonne of carbon, hold them for a few months as the price went up, then sell them to Black Coal Power Station Ltd., England, for $25.

This would allow Black Coal Ltd. to pump out an extra million tons of carbon dioxide into the atmosphere and pass on the cost of the credits it had just bought to its electricity consumers. This subsidised the electricity generated by Acme Wind Farm to the tune of $20 million while making the electricity generated by Black Coal $25 million more expensive. Clean Sky would pocket the 20 per cent profit on the sale of the credits. Everyone was happy, that is except the poor householder who had to foot the bill for this hocus-pocus.

All in all the profit on a $25 million trade could be a cool $5 million and nothing had actually been manufactured. There were no stocks, no transport costs; essentially the product he was selling didn't really exist. Robin had become Clean Sky's golden boy. Commission on each trade was 50 per cent of gross profit – he was laughing all the way to the Caymans.

CHAPTER 18

It had been a long night. After Connie's two-hour stint on laptop duty, she had retired, dejected, to one of the guestrooms that Cheryl had made up. It was good to have a room to herself again. Randolph's snoring had to be heard to be believed. But to be fair to him; he had turned out to be much more than a godfather; he had been a godsend over the last few days. She could not conceive how she would have made it through without him.

While Cheryl's fear had overwhelmed what Randolph had assured Connie was a very hospitable personality, Ruairi on the other hand added to her support system. These two old soldiers gave her a warm fuzzy feeling; they must have been a hell of a team in their day. Daylight was coming through the window. Connie leapt out of bed and headed for the kitchen bumping into Cheryl as she did so.

'Why didn't you wake me? I was due back on watch hours ago.'

'You were dead to the world. Anyway, the toy soldiers are enjoying being back in the saddle, plotting and scheming; happy as pigs in muck, they are.

You'd hardly know there was some psychopathic assassin out there trying to kill us, would you?'

The contempt in her voice was tangible; Cheryl was not warming to Connie, nor she to her.

'What time is it?'

'Nearly nine. Breakfast's on the table. No news from lover-boy, I'm afraid.' She did not even try to hide her lack of sincerity.

Connie dressed quickly and ran down the stairs to the kitchen. The three of them were tucking into a traditional farmhouse breakfast with all the trimmings.

'God, I didn't know sitting watching a computer screen could give you such an appetite,' quipped Ruairi.

'Who's watching it now?'

'Only just stepped away from it, pet.'

'When did you last refresh?'

'Just five minutes ago. Now sit down and get some good old-fashioned home cooking into you. It'll set you up for the day. He's made us wait all night; now he can wait a few minutes.'

Connie wanted to go straight into the drawing room but boy, that fry-up smelled good. She piled on fried eggs, bacon and toast, picked up the plate and took it in to the computer. As she sat down, balancing the plate on her knee, she almost tipped it onto the floor in her excitement as the salutation popped up.

'*Hi there, Sweetpie, had a good sleep?*'

'He's back, he's back,' she screamed across the house.

The others came rushing in. The communication with Seth was taking on the air of a séance. There was a distinct feeling of something otherworldly bridging the void between the farmhouse and – who knows where. They waited with bated breath for another tap on the floor, another cryptic missive that might shed light on the reason for their current state of limbo.

'Weather's taken a turn for the worse; but nothing like that last trip to New York, temperature dropped to 53 degrees Fahrenheit (whatever that is in real money) in midsummer. Can you believe it and with a north wind blowing it was like winter. The chicks on the street downtown were freezing their butts off. God, the way they dress, real gaol bate, you know the age of consent is higher over there, though, not that I would have any interest in them. You're still the only one for me; you know that, don't you? I'll never forget when you got that old Peugeot 104 for your 21st birthday. God, you looked fantastic. I hope you're ready for the next time Mr Tumnus comes down to visit the forest to hide a little something in the fairy pocket. Got to go now. Talk to you again tomorrow.'

'That's it? That's the message – but what the hell does it mean?' Connie was flummoxed.

'You tell us; it's all about what you and he got up to or didn't as the case may be.' Cheryl smirked.

'Well, for a start I didn't get a car for my 21st birthday and I have never owned a Peugeot 104 and we didn't even know each other when I turned 21.'

'Right, so something is hidden there. What about the rest?' said Randolph.

To break the tension Ruairi found it necessary to state the obvious. 'We know he wasn't in New York from the last message, so he is trying to tell us something using the temperature?'

'Could it be an address?' Randolph started frantically jotting down numbers. 'I think it's a map reference – a lat. long.'

'What do you mean?' Connie had never been into map reading.

'He's mentioned two points of the compass.'

'No, he hasn't; he just mentioned north.'

'Look, he talks about the age of consent being higher over there – America is west of here.'

'Bit of a long shot, don't you think?'

'Not if you combine it with the rest of the message. He's giving us a lot of numbers, 53, 104, 21. Can we make a stab at the lat. long.?'

'Will you stop saying that? What the hell does latlong mean?'

'Latitude and longitude: so many degrees north or south of the equator – north in this case – and so many degrees east or west of the Greenwich meridian. What I'm seeing here is 53 degrees north – he gives just one number before he mentions north – and then two numbers 104 and 21 before he mentions west.'

'I'll just put that into Google Earth to see where it is.'

'No, stop!' Randolph grabbed Connie's wrist and jerked it away from the keyboard, producing a yelp from the startled girl.

'What did you do that for? It really hurt!'

'Sorry, I'm really sorry. It's just that if anyone is monitoring our Internet connection and they see us punching in map references, it will give them a good idea of what we're up to. It wouldn't take them too long to realise that Tony is actually Seth.'

A cold shiver ran down Connie's spine. She had almost given away the location of her beloved. But there was something else bothering her; she couldn't quite put her finger on it.

'Either of you got a satnav?' Randolph looked hopefully at Cheryl and Ruairi.

'I have a TomTom in the car; I'll go get it.'

Randolph turned to Ruairi. 'While Cheryl is getting the satnav, I can tell you straight away that it can't be 104 degrees 21 minutes west, as that would be in the middle of the Pacific, so we need to look at the numbers a little more closely. Now this could be 10 degrees 4 minutes 21 seconds west – I reckon that would put him somewhere on the far west coast of Ireland. What do you think, Ruairi? You're from Galway. Isn't that in your neck of the woods?'

'Could be, could be. Let's put it in. Give us that machine here, Cheryl.'

Ruairi tapped in the coordinates and hit OK. The TomTom responded with:

'No useable locations near cursor.'

'Anyone know what that means?'

'I think it means you're in the sea. Just as a test put in 9 degrees west and see where you end up.'

Ruairi ran the numbers again.

'Puts us just north of Ennis; you're right, Randy, 10 degrees would put him in the Atlantic, just off the Aran Islands. Any more bright ideas?'

'Let's shift the decimal place one more time.'

'Give it to me, Randolph.'

'Let's see, 1 degree 04 minutes 21 seconds. Where would that put him?'

'Oh yes, that's more like it – East Midlands airport.'

'What, is he leaving the country? What's he trying to tell us?' Connie looked panicked.

The thought of Seth just upping sticks and fleeing Britain had never occurred to her. How could he possibly abandon her?

'Wait, hang on a minute. This looks a bit odd. If he is giving us a very specific location, then it's on the grass just off one of the runways. Why would he do that?'

'The rest of the message suggests that he is hiding something for us to find. Maybe that is the location,' Ruairi suggested.

'Bit of an odd place to leave something. For a start, passengers are not allowed air-side. If we were to go waltzing down the runway, we would be picked up in no time. I think 53 is too round a number for a latitude anyway. Is there anything else unusual about the message that might give us a clue as to what and where he might hide something?' Randolph looked perplexed.

All eyes turned to Connie. The colour started at her neck and moved swiftly up her cheeks until her face was bright crimson.

'What? Come on – spit it out. We are all adults here, been at it a lot longer than you two. How come the young think they are the only ones who ever had sex?'

'Well…'

She paused. Ruairi was enjoying her discomfort. He could hardly contain himself – there was nothing so sexy as a girl consumed by her own embarrassment. She started again.

'…He refers to Mr Tumnus visiting the forest…' They all knew what was coming but they wanted to hear her say it. 'I wax…everything.'

'So what you're saying is, there's no forest for Mr Tumnus to visit.' Cheryl let out a guffaw.

The two men just stood, alone with their own thoughts.

'Thanks for your sensitivity, everyone, but it's a strong clue. Maybe he means a real forest.'

'Maybe he doesn't like you waxing,' quipped Cheryl.

'Enough already, can't you two get on? I think Ruairi's right. We're still missing some numbers. What does he say before he mentions the north wind?'

'"Whatever that is in real money" – anyone know what 53 degrees Fahrenheit is in Centigrade?'

'Good one. From my school days, if I remember correctly, you subtract 32 and divide by 1.8. I'll let you do that for me, Connie.'

'It's 11.66 recurring so it could be 11 or 12.'

'Let's assume he rounded up and call it 53 degrees 12 minutes north. What does that give us,

Ruairi?'

After a short pause and gradually raising eyebrows Ruairi declared, 'I think we have it, or very close – middle of a ploughed field just to the left of – wait for it…'

'Stop messing, Ruairi, just tell us.'

'…Sherwood Forest. There's your forest, girl.'

'You've got to be kidding me. That's only about 10 miles away. How could he possibly have known where we were?' Randolph was gobsmacked.

'He couldn't; it's just serendipity, about the only bit of good luck we have had these last few days.' Connie was beaming.

'I'm not sure it's blind chance. If Seth had wanted to get something to us, a good place to put it would be in the middle of the country. Then the average distance we would have to travel from any point would only be half the length or breadth. We are almost in the dead centre; they don't call this the Midlands for nothing.'

'But shit, 10 miles away – we must have done something good in a previous life to deserve this.'

'Hey, hold your horses, we're not there yet, Cheryl. The latitude only gives us degrees and minutes, the longitude gives us degrees minutes and seconds. I think we're still missing a number. Now come on everyone, thinking caps on. What other number is hiding in the message – think sex, a bit more innuendo, if you please.' Ruairi was really into the swing.

Once again everyone looked to Connie for

inspiration but none was forthcoming.

'Never mind. I've got it. It's 17.'

'Where's that?'

'Age of consent in New York State is 17 years. He says, "you know the age of consent is higher over there".'

'Just the sort of thing you would know. Randy by name, Randy by nature.'

'Oh, like I've never heard that one before. Just put the figure in. Let's see what the Lord has sent us.'

'Hmm, it's on a road this time – Broad Drive, that rings a bell, near Edwinstowe.' Ruairi's brow furrowed.

'Well, well, and you don't know what's there, you the great backwoods man. You should be ashamed of yourself. You take just about everyone who comes to visit us to see it. I'm sick of the place myself but I now know where Mr Tumnus has hidden his little something.' Cheryl folded her arms in an exaggerated smug gesture.

'Of course, "the Major Oak". We've cracked it, Randy. Now that's what I call a joint effort.'

'But if it's in a tree, whatever Seth has hidden could be anywhere, and I presume that by the name, this is a big tree.' Connie was sceptical.

'You've obviously never visited, have you? 'Cos if you had, you would know there was only one place to hide anything and that would be in the great big hole in the middle of the old sucker.'

'What are we waiting for? Let's go get it.'

'I don't know what you are waiting for but let

me tell you, girly pie, you and Randy are not going anywhere. Your pictures are all over the TV and the papers. It would be madness for you to step outside the door. No, Cheryl and I will go and retrieve whatever it is; you stay here and keep an eye on the computer, just in case he calls back.'

'He's right, Connie, we need to lie low. No point in exposing ourselves to any unnecessary danger. Anyway, if Tao is watching, we might provoke some response if he sees us on the move again. Best let Ruairi and Cheryl do some shopping and take a little walk in the woods on the way home. I suggest you do the standard dry cleaning, Ruairi, but if they are as good as I think they are, I don't think you'll lose them. Just make the whole thing look casual.'

'Oh yeah, like we would just take off for a walk in the woods when we have got a couple of fugitives staying with us.'

'OK, I take your point, but is there any legitimate reason why you might need to visit the area? I don't know, something to do with the farm, collect wood, hunt deer, whatever you farmers do?'

'Not a bad idea. We could hitch up a trailer and pretend to drop something off in the park, fence posts or the like; if Cheryl stayed in the Land Rover that would split any tail. It's into tourist season now and a Saturday to boot so the place will be heaving. With any luck I could lose a tail for a few minutes while I make the pickup. Let's give it a shot.'

CHAPTER 19

'The residents have left in a farm vehicle.'
'Follow them. Van Klaveren and the girl, are they definitely still in the house?'
'Yes, we have eyes on them.'
'Keep the bulk of your men at the farm.'
'As you wish.'

The single pursuit car had little difficulty keeping the McElhattons in sight. First call was the local newsagents, where Cheryl picked up a copy of the *Daily Mail* and some milk, trying to maintain an air of normality. The Land Rover and trailer pulled away again and in typical farm-vehicle style had soon created a snake of frustrated road users. Staying four cars back, it became obvious that the couple were not attempting to make a run for it, nor were they using any form of surveillance evasion.

Tao had employed the best in the business when it came to covert surveillance and the quarry was acting with all the misplaced confidence of amateurs. The snake wound its way north and very soon became embroiled in a traffic jam not of its own making. The cars ahead appeared to be mainly day trippers. The heads of children and the occasional dog hung out of car windows, variously pulling faces and making gestures at the passing traffic before suddenly being yanked out of sight by an unseen force. A multitude of brown signposts pointing in the direction of travel of the throng offered delights such as parks, cafés and souvenirs, each one prefaced with the two words: 'Sherwood Forest'. Making an educated guess, the tail radioed back the likely destination.

'Probably the Sherwood Forest Country Park, boss; they have fence posts and wire in the trailer – looks like a drop off.'

'Keep on them. It could be a feint, but I doubt it.'

Soon the convoy was pulling into the park, confirming the suspicions of those following. Not wishing to get caught up in the car park melee, the men eased the vehicle onto the grass verge, midway between entrance and exit, keeping both in sight. Fifteen minutes passed before they spotted the Land Rover and trailer exiting the park sans fence posts, heading back in the direction of the farm. Once out of sight, the car performed a U-turn and, keeping a good distance, tailed them back to Harlow Wood; just one more tedious and repetitive part of an average surveillance operation.

* * * * *

The men were in the kitchen talking in hushed tones while Cheryl leafed through the newspaper in the lounge looking for anything useful that the investigative reporters might have unearthed about the Franks case. Prime among them was Jack Mates who had been the major contributor in the Mail since the story broke. Connie was totally absorbed plugging in the memory stick retrieved from the Major Oak and copying all the files left by Seth. Confident that he would not be overheard, Ruairi confided in Randolph.

'We were followed. I'm sure of it.'

'What makes you think that?'

'Well, I didn't see them actually following us but this car just stood out from all the others. Look, the place was jammers. No one in their right mind who wasn't a fan of Robin Hood and his merry men would have been caught dead in that area on a Saturday morning in the summer. A Grey Ford Mondeo with two men in it was parked on the grass between the entrance and the exit of the park. As we drove past, they seemed to be looking at a map. Who the fuck uses a map these days? It's all satnav. These buckos need to up their trade craft.'

'Yeh, I think you're right. Don't mention it to the girls; they're spooked enough as it is. All it does is confirm what we suspected in the first place.'

'Do you think they followed you to the tree?

'No, not a chance, they didn't even enter the car park. It seems your ruse of delivering the fence posts fooled them. While I made the collection, Cheryl unloaded them and stacked them against a tree. They'll probably still be there in 10 years.'

'You know, boy, that Cheryl of yours, she's a horse of a woman.' Randolph delivered this line in a comic Cork accent, provoking a peal of laughter from Ruairi.

'What's going on in there, you two? Having a laugh at my expense, are you?'

'No, no, dear, utterly complementary. I was just telling Randy how strong you are.' This remark generated more hilarity in the two men.

'Bugger you both. Get in here and let's come up with a quick confirmation to Seth that we got the package.'

With all the elation at getting the other half of the puzzle, they had forgotten that Seth was waiting for them.

'Let's be careful now. We don't want to get sloppy and start giving the game away. Keep up the innuendo and the double entendre, Connie. You're doing great,' Randolph said encouragingly.

'I think I could make a profession out of this. I'm beginning to like it.'

'Don't get carried away – I only said you were great; I didn't say you were John le Carré.'

'Well, it's easy to let him know we have the stick – he has written "soup" in pen on the plastic. I presume he wants us to use the word to indicate we have it. How about *'I'm just going to make some soup. Would you like some?'* That's utterly banal. No one could possibly read anything into that.'

'OK, blast that off. We don't know when he will have to leave wherever he is transmitting from.'

'Transmitting! You make it sound as though he's a ham radio operator. Get with the lingo, Daddy O.' Connie stroked the keys once again. Seth's response was instantaneous.

'Delicious, said Max.'

'Eh?'

'Your children are probably too old for *Max's First Words*, Ruairi. It's from a kiddie's book. I remember it and so does Seth.'

'Oh wonderful. Does that help us any?' Cheryl chipped in.

'No, not really.'

'Then tell him to stop pissing about and send us something useful.'

'I don't think you are being fair, Cheryl. I take that message as an acknowledgement that he understands we have picked up his message. He'll be surprised that we got it so quickly; he could have no idea that we are so close to Sherwood Forest. Do you realise what this also means? Seth must also be nearby; this is both a blessing and a curse. It's critical that he does not make any attempt to see Connie. In fact, we need to let him know that we are being watched.'

'But we can't be sure. Wouldn't it be so much better if we could discuss what to say to the press with him?'

The look of hope in Connie's eyes would have melted the hardest of hearts.

'But, pet, the only thing keeping us and him from the grim reaper is the fact that Tao can't get to him. We have to stay strong. We need to focus on getting this message to the BBC bloke and we need to do it today. Now let's sign off from Seth. Where he is and what he thinks are just a distraction. We have what we need. Let's get to it.'

∗ ∗ ∗ ∗ ∗

Good God! How in the name of Jesus did they get the memory stick so quickly? Seth sat back in amazement when the invitation to take a cup of soup was extended. Then it hit him. At the most, Connie must only be 30 miles away; they needn't have gone through this pantomime at all – he could have delivered it to her. She must have worked that out as well; they needed to arrange a meet. He was about to send a message when he was stopped dead in his tracks.

'Shit Pot, I only have eyes for you but if I don't keep an eye on this soup I might spill some, like I did in New York, and you know then the waiter nearly killed me when he saw it go on the carpet. Got to go now, talk again soon.'

It was clear to Seth that Connie was warning him off. So she needed to focus on the contents of the memory stick, but what was this about Tao? What did Tao see – did he see her pick up the chip? But if he did, how come she still had it? Was he watching her? A guy could go crazy trying to fathom this. Connie did not want to meet him; she was going to work on the story and he was to back off, that much he was sure of.

If Tao was watching her, he was also monitoring her computer and by definition anyone who was communicating with her, which meant him. He needed to leave this place and not return, he just prayed that they had not caught up with him. No, that couldn't be the case. There was no way because if they had, he would already be dead and so would Connie.

* * * * *

While Connie and Randolph collated the details that Seth had sent them and wove it into their own narrative, Ruairi and Cheryl set about devising a plan to contact Anthony Thoroughgood. How would they get him interested without 'the listeners' finding out what they were up to? Any attempt to email or telephone him would likely bring retribution of one sort or another, but it was imperative to get the story out if they were to return to anything approaching normality.

'What about writing to him? If we move quickly we could have a letter in the last post and he would have it by Monday. Who would suspect that we would try to contact the press using good old snail mail?' Cheryl was ever the practical one.

'As I have always said, you are not just a pretty face, but I have a better idea. As time is of the essence, why don't we include the memory chip and just stick in a covering letter, so to speak.'

'But what if it is intercepted, then Tao would know we know everything and our lives would be worth squat.'

'Hmm, good point; but then how do we get him interested enough to blow the whistle on Seth's story, which would release Seth as well as telling Randy and Connie's tale, which would release them?'

'Why not split the information, just like it was for us, split between Seth and Connie.'

'How do you mean?'

'Send one half of the information to one journalist and the other half to another; if Tao intercepts one piece, he won't think we have the full story. Then all we have to do is get the two journalists to talk to each other.'

'Oh, is that all? Should be a piece of piss, then.'

'Who would you suggest as the second journalist?'

'Well,' Cheryl chipped in, 'Anthony Thoroughgood is an environmental correspondent and would know all about what Seth has sent to us so why not contact a crime correspondent like Jack Mates of the *Daily Mail*? He has been reporting on the murder of Franks. He would give his eye teeth to get his hands on the inside story.'

'I like it, I like it; but how do we get them to talk to each other without giving the game away?'

CHAPTER 20

Anthony Thoroughgood was contemplating the significant milestone that was the big 4-0 as he began the week, by way of the daily dice with death across four lanes of St Peter's Street. It was a shortcut from Leeds City Bus station to the glossy steel and glass Broadcasting Centre, home to BBC Yorkshire. Rounding the corner to the rear of the edifice, his nose was assailed by the heady mix of herbs and spices wafting from the Aagrah Indian restaurant bizarrely located at the front of the building under the giant BBC Yorkshire banner, somewhat implying that the BBC had gone into the catering business. Bowling through the revolving door, he was propelled up to the front desk where he enquired, 'Any post this fine morning, Janet?'

'Only the usual invites to invest in "not to be missed" foreign property opportunities and this brown envelope marked private and confidential, in a lady's hand, I'll wager – no doubt a payoff from your latest blackmail scam.'

Janet would put a spring in anyone's step, he thought, even on an early Monday morning.

'Thanks, me duck.'

Already his day was brightening and worries of being a 40-something were fading from his mind. Taking the lift to the third floor, he dumped the post on his desk and wandered down to the coffee machine to chew the fat and earwig on any office gossip. The topic of the day was once again the murder of a senior policewoman in Norwich. The red tops were having a field day with their barely disguised xenophobic editorials.

Back at his desk, with a caffeine fix already coursing through his veins, he opened the mystery item of mail. While his curiosity had been initially aroused by the handwritten address (one so rarely received hand-addressed envelopes these days), the opening paragraph got off to a bad start.

> Dear Jack,

> In relation to your article in Friday's paper on the murder of police Inspector Franks, I would like to…

It was immediately apparent that the sender had placed the document in the wrong envelope. He was a radio and TV reporter, he did not write for the rags and he certainly did not sully his hands with gruesome tabloid sensation stories. He flicked over the sheet expecting it to be signed 'Appalled of Headingly' but his jaw dropped as he read

> Yours sincerely, Constance Bennett.

Perhaps this was some kind of practical joke? He quickly turned back to the beginning of the letter and began to read with growing incredulity the inside story of the life and death of Inspector Franks. Details were included that had not been reported on either the television or in the newspapers. This was a cry for help, but how could she have made such an astounding error in sending it to him? The letter was clearly aimed at a tabloid reporter whom she hoped would break the story and in so doing, release her from the grip of the Chinese mafia. But he, Anthony Thoroughgood, was not the man to do it. He needed to find out who this Jack was and make contact.

He ran down to the press room where copies of all national and local papers were delivered daily. It was the job of an office nobody to trawl through them looking for any story that the Beeb might have missed and pass it on to whoever had slack in their schedule. Starting with the red tops, he began to check the by-lines of journalists writing about the Inspector's murder the previous Friday. It was not long before he identified Jack Mates of the *Daily Mail* as the Jack referred to in the letter from Ms Bennett. Rushing over to his secretary, he was about to ask her to put in a call to Mates when she said, 'There's a call for you, Anthony. The guy says it's very urgent – won't give his name. Will I tell him you're out?'

'No, Bess, put him through to my desk.'

The voice at the other end was very insistent and commanding but there was a slight tremble to his words.

'I have something of yours and I believe you may have something of mine. Don't ask any questions. Leave your office, find the nearest public call box and ring this number in 10 minutes.'

The caller gave out a number, repeated it, then the line went dead. Anthony's head was swimming. He couldn't take in all that was coming at him. Everything was moving too fast. If it was who he thought it was, then he suspected that the letter he had received had been no mistake. A similar 'mistake' had been made with a letter for him being sent to Jack Mates.

But why would someone suspected of murder, trying to clear their name, be playing such complicated games and why would Jack Mates go to such lengths to hide his identity, unless the fears expressed in Bennett's letter in relation to the involvement of Chinese organised crime were true? Thoroughgood bundled up the papers, put them back in the brown envelope and locked them in his desk.

After a moment's hesitation, he unlocked the desk, took out the envelope and walked over to the next desk, which had been left vacant since the previous occupant had been shown the door during recent 'restructuring'. He opened one of the drawers, empty save for a few sweet papers and old Visa receipts. Making sure no one was looking; he slipped in the envelope and locked the desk with the set of two keys dutifully left hanging in the lock. Maybe he was being paranoid but...

Striding over to the lift, he jabbed the call button a few times before taking to the stairs. On his way through the foyer, he shouted over his shoulder to Janet that he was just going out for a few minutes and he would be back soon.

* * * * *

Mates stood in the call box on High Street Kensington, his heart pounding. He was taking a big risk contacting Thoroughgood. If Whitten was right and the Tong were on his tail, they might already know about Thoroughgood and be monitoring his calls, as they could be monitoring his own.

Thirty years of tracking down gangsters had taught him to always err on the side of caution. Most of his colleagues had moved to anonymous pay-as-you-go mobile phones to conduct sensitive conversations. Mates simply hadn't moved with the times, partly because he was not convinced that they were that secure and partly because he was a cheapskate and knew that he would be tempted to re-use them and therein lay disaster.

After 30 minutes had passed, he knew that Thoroughgood was not going to ring. Could he have misunderstood? Could he simply have thought it was a crank call and ignored it? Would he try again, perhaps giving a little more information this time, a little carrot to draw him out, but what could he say that would not possibly put them both in jeopardy? His fingers hovered over the keypad. He dialled again.

'Please hold while we try to connect you. Your call is important to us. An operator will be with you shortly.'

The hold music droned on interminably, which was odd; the BBC usually answered very quickly. He dropped the line and tried again: same thing. He got a cold feeling in his gut. He hung up the receiver and headed for the train station.

* * * * *

Sitting in Reception, Janet heard the bang, then a few seconds later the screams, followed by people running down the road towards the bus station. It was a traffic accident for sure. She struggled with herself; it was ingrained in her not to leave the switch unattended but she was trained in first aid and CPR.

'To hell with it.'

She rushed out of the building and ran towards the small knot of people gathered at the side of the road. The railings, preventing pedestrians from straying onto the dual carriageway, were bent over onto the pavement. She could make out a pair of legs twisted back on themselves at an unnatural angle. An upright from the railings had broken free and was sticking out of the chest of the lifeless body. The scene was horrific; all her training could do nothing for this man. She was about to turn away when an identity badge lying in the middle of the road caught her eye; the traffic had stopped so she picked her way through the tangled wreckage of the barrier and retrieved it. Turning it over, her legs became rooted to the spot as she read the familiar name. She turned back to the crash scene. He was unrecognisable; the impact with the vehicle had so rearranged his features that not even his mother would have known him. A member of the crowd walked over and put a comforting arm around her shoulder.

'Did you know him, deary?' Not getting an answer, the woman felt compelled to fill the silence. 'I saw what 'appened, you know? 'E'd 'opped the barrier and was tryin' to cross when this van, this sort of square-looking thing with all its windows blacked out, it swerved across the road and crushed 'im against the barrier. It didn't stop, the little bastard, 'e just carried on. Must 'ave panicked, I suppose. Driver won't get far, though, smashed up all 'is wing, 'e did. But 'e shouldn't 'ave jumped the barrier, poor lamb, that's what it's there for – such a dangerous road...'

Her voice trailed off. Getting no response, she slowly withdrew her arm and wandered off to tell her story to someone a little more responsive. Janet stood alone in a state of shock as the impact of Anthony's death sank in.

* * * * *

'How long do you think it will take them to get together and break the story?'

Connie was optimistic, but Randolph less so.

'God knows, and he's not telling. Having said that, neither of these men is stupid; each story by itself is enough to get the juices of these hacks flowing. The fact that they have clearly got a document meant for someone else will only make it that much more intriguing. As to whether they will work out who the other guy is – if you're in the trade, hmm, I don't think it should be too difficult. Now it's just a waiting game. We have done everything we can.'

With bated breath Randolph and Constance sat around the computer on Monday morning, praying for a quick release from the torture of waiting. Ruairi and Cheryl busied themselves with jobs around the farm – at least they had something to keep them occupied. By midday they had tired of monitoring the news feeds and Randolph switched on the television to catch the one o'clock news in a vain hope that they may have picked up something that the Internet had not. The headlines helped to relieve the tedium of the morning's vigil, but as the bulletin was drawing to a close

'…*and in local news, the BBC is in mourning today after the tragic death of their environmental correspondent, Anthony Thoroughgood, killed in a traffic accident outside the BBC's northern headquarters in Leeds. Colleagues said of Anthony…*'

'Dear God, they got him.'

Still pouring over the computer, Constance

was distracted. 'What did you say, Randy?'

'I said Tao got him, killed in a hit and run.'

'Got who, goddamn it? Got who?' The panic in Constance had transformed her voice in a sudden piercing shriek.

'Thoroughgood. They've killed Thoroughgood.' His voice was low and monotone as though all the stuffing had been knocked out of him.

Connie didn't know whether to laugh or cry. For a split second she thought Randy had meant Seth. There was a brief moment of relief followed by a shocking wave of depression as the full implications of what he had said hit home. They had failed. Somehow the letters had been tracked and with ruthless efficiency, Tao had executed Thoroughgood; no doubt Mates would quickly follow – if he was not dead already. Not only had they failed but, through their bungling, they had been directly responsible for the deaths of at least one of these men. Connie's head dropped and she stared at the keyboard, for a moment her fingers were stuck to the keys, her body unresponsive. Ruairi stuck his head around the door of the drawing room.

'What's up?'

Neither of them spoke. Randolph rewound the Sky+ box and replayed the news article. Ruairi's face fell.

'Well, that's a blow – poor bastard. Best put our thinking caps on then and come up with a new plan. No sense in crying over spilt milk.'

His sanguine approach to the journalist's death was more than Connie could take and she rushed past him, out of the door and up the stairs to her bedroom.

'Took it hard, then, did she?'

Randy nodded. 'Took it pretty hard myself. Where the hell do we go from here?'

* * * * *

'He was contacted, possibly by van Klaveren; we are still waiting for confirmation of the voice pattern.'

'Why did you kill him now?' Yat-sen suppressed his anger.

'He was moving to a pubic call box so we would not have been able to monitor the conversation. I ordered the van to take him out.'

'It was a risk, Tao, but the police seem confident that it was an accident. The van is safe?'

'The equipment is being transferred as we speak. Soon it will be destroyed.'

'Let me know when you have confirmation of the voice print. We need to know if it was van Klaveren who made the call and if not, who it was.'

This latest development had raised the stakes. The couple were proving to be unexpectedly resourceful. The time was approaching when their usefulness was about to be outweighed by their danger to the organisation.

* * * * *

The London–Leeds express took just over two hours so Mates was in Leeds before lunch. The taxi dropped him off outside Broadcasting Centre; he paid the driver and entered through the revolving door. The receptionist looked puffy eyed and if he didn't know better, he would have thought she had been crying.

'Jack Mates of the *Daily Mail* to see Anthony Thoroughgood – he's expecting me.'

This sort of bluff rolled off his silver tongue as it had for the past 30 years. Often the girls on the desk didn't even bother to check and would send him straight up. On this occasion the reaction both shocked and terrified him. The sudden tears were followed by an apology and a brave attempt to compose herself. The stumbling explanation of Thoroughgood's untimely death was made all the more poignant by the pathetic detail of his final words.

'He said he was only popping out for a few minutes and would be back soon.'

Thinking on his feet, Mates embellished the lie.

'We were working on a big story together – I sent him a package. Do you know if he got it?'

If his hunch was right and Thoroughgood had received a similar letter to his own, it was worth taking a flyer.

'Oh, it was you, was it? We joked about it being a payoff.' A faint smile crossed her tear-stained face. 'He was a lovely man, you know.'

'He was also a true friend.'

If there was one thing Mates was good at, it was faking sincerity. He leaned over the desk in a conspiratorial manner.

'It's important that those papers don't fall into the wrong hands. Lives depend on it.'

God, that sounded corny, but he could not come up with anything better on the spur of the moment, and anyway, it was true; his own life depended on it.

'Look, I'll get his secretary to bring it down to you. He didn't have it with him when he died.'

The tears welled up again as she said the words, but she held it together and rang through.

'Elizabeth, I've a friend of Anthony's down here in reception. He needs a letter from his desk; he says it's very important. All right.' She replaced the receiver.

'Elizabeth will drop down and talk to you. If you'd like to wait over there, she'll be with you in a moment.'

It was clear the secretary was not going to be such a pushover. Every minute he hung around this building he was increasing his chances of being associated with Thoroughgood, if that link had not been made already. He toyed with the idea of slipping out of the offices and making a run for it, but before he could make up his mind the lift doors opened and a girl walked towards him with a purposeful and somewhat hostile manner. He stood up as she approached and took out his press ID card.

'My name is Jack Mates of the *Daily Mail.*'

As he spoke a flicker of recognition played

across the girl's face; the red-rimmed eyes testified to the popularity of the recently deceased, at least with the ladies anyway.

'It was *you* he spoke to this morning just before he left the office, wasn't it? What did you say to him? Why wouldn't you give your name?'

'Because Anthony's calls were being monitored. He was on the way to a call box to ring me when he was murdered.'

'What do you mean "murdered"; the police said it was an accident?' The pitch of her voice began to rise as the stress started to kick in.

'Keep your voice down or you'll get us both killed.' This bald statement pulled her up short and any animosity that she might have been harbouring towards him turned into shocked disbelief. Mates decided to play hard ball.

'Look, Anthony has a document of mine and I need to get it back before anyone else sees it. Take me up to his desk. I'll show you the contents. If it's not written to me, I'll walk away, but if it is, I'm taking it with me and you never saw me. OK?'

The girl seemed mesmerised; his decision to sock it to her had paid off. He followed her to the lift and up to the third floor. They remained silent as she led him over to the unprepossessing desk in a row of similar workstations. She unlocked the desk with her master key and they both went through the sorry remains of all that was left of a 10-year career at the BBC.

'It's not here.'

'I can see that. Where else could he have put

it?'

'I don't know. This is his desk – it's where he kept everything.'

'This stuff was dynamite, right? He must have hidden it somewhere.'

Mates began to feel around under the lip of each drawer, to see if Thoroughgood had taped the document to the underside of the desk. He came up empty. Between taking his call and heading down to the phone box he would have had very little time to secrete the envelope. Casting around for some clue as to its whereabouts, his eyes fell on a set of keys in the top drawer.

'What are these keys for?'

'They are his desk keys.'

'I doubt it. His drawers were locked. You unlocked them with your key, so why would he have locked his own keys in the desk?'

Mates tried one of the two identical keys in the desk and as he suspected, the lock would not turn.

'What other desk could these be for? Did he have another desk?'

'No, that's all he was allocated. No one has two desks.'

He looked at the next workstation. It was clearly abandoned. Boxes of cardboard cups were pushed in behind the swivel chair and two large copies of the *Yellow Pages*, still in their plastic wrappers, were dumped on top. Removing the keys from Thoroughgood's desk, he inserted one of them into the lock of the adjoining desk. The key turned and in the top drawer, lying in the dust, was an identical brown envelope to the one he had received that morning. His hunch was correct. Removing the contents, he turned to the secretary.

'Look as I said—' She cut him off mid-sentence.

'I don't want to see. Just take it and get out of here; you're scaring the bejesus out of me.'

Stuffing the papers into his jacket pocket, he headed for the lifts. He couldn't believe he had pulled it off. God, he was good! Thirty years in the game and he had lost none of the finesse. He had just committed a criminal offence and so had Elizabeth. Knowing what he did, that Thoroughgood had been murdered, he should have gone straight to the police. Instead he had stolen vital evidence from the murder victim and involved the poor man's secretary in a conspiracy. Now what would he do for the rest of the day?

As he left the building, he was on alert for any suspicious characters that might be taking too much interest in him; particularly anyone with an Oriental look about them. The foyer was clear and when he turned left onto the street, the place was deserted. Walking down the alley at the back of the BBC, he carried on through the car park, his heart pounding in his chest. At any moment he expected to be jumped by some Boxer assassin. As he rounded the Playhouse, he was once again on St Peter's Street. He hailed a taxi on the Eastgate roundabout and directed him to the train station.

As he lay back in the cab, he clutched the

brown envelope that had cost Thoroughgood his life. The document that Mates received that had been meant for Thoroughgood had been sensational. How could the document meant for him top that?

He withdrew the introductory letter from his pocket and it opened on the back page. The signature was as he expected – the police were right. Deep Cool and Connie Bennett were somehow connected. The same guy that was trying to kill Seth Whitten was also trying to kill the most wanted woman in England and the two of them had managed to get the whole story of their plight to him. He didn't know whether to be flattered or terrified. If they had not been supremely careful, and by the untimely demise of the BBC correspondent they clearly had not, he had just been placed in the frame with them.

CHAPTER 21

The mood in the farmhouse was dour. Connie had not left her room in over an hour, in which time the rest of the household had consumed half a bottle of Jameson's. The door to the lounge opened slowly and Connie's forlorn face peered around the edge.

'It was me. I'm responsible.'

'Responsible for what?' Cheryl was sharp. She was sick of treating everyone with kid gloves. The house was probably surrounded by a bunch of coldblooded killers and Connie was mooning around the place like some jilted lover. Who gave a crap what she was responsible for? They could all be dead in the morning.

'Anthony Thoroughgood – I caused his death. I have been up in my room wracking my brains as to how Tao could possibly have intercepted the letters and identified Thoroughgood and Mates. Then I realised he didn't need to. I gave him Thoroughgood's name when I googled his details yesterday. We're fairly sure Tao is monitoring our communications and I think this proves it.'

'We all sat there and let you do it. Perhaps there's a ray of hope after all. If Tao did not get to

Thoroughgood by intercepting the letters, then maybe he still doesn't know about Mates. If our original plan worked there's even a chance that Thoroughgood and Mates got in touch, in which case maybe Mates has enough to go to press.'

'Come on, Ruairi, I think you're clutching at straws here. Thoroughgood was killed this morning. What's the likelihood that the two men would have been able to work out who the letters were for and get in contact before Thoroughgood was killed?' Cheryl was negative as usual.

'No, wait a minute. Ruairi could be right,' said Randolph. 'Why kill Thoroughgood now, why not yesterday or tomorrow? The Tong are hardly likely to kill a BBC correspondent just because we googled him. Something must have precipitated the killing. The report said he died in a hit and run; therefore he must have been outside the BBC. It was too late in the morning for him to be arriving at work so he was on his way somewhere – perhaps to meet with Mates.'

'But the bad news is that Tao must have intercepted his phone calls to know that Thoroughgood was onto something, in which case they know who Mates is and if he is not already dead, then he soon will be.'

'Mates is an investigative journalist. He must have known that what we have given him is dynamite. I think he will have protected himself. Thoroughgood was just an environment correspondent and we had already placed him in the cross hairs. As soon as Mates heard about Thoroughgood's death he will have gone to ground. Unless the Tong were already tracking him, which they would have had no reason to, there is no way they are going to find him easily.'

'But unless Mates has both documents, which I doubt, then any attempt to publish will go off half cocked. We gave him only the global warming side of the story. Nobody knows who Seth is. It would just be another boring global warming conspiracy theory. He needs to know that Franks' death is integral to what has been going on and that we are being hunted by the Tong.'

'Not so fast. He may not need to know about our involvement. If he is any sort of a hack he will have put two and two together and realised that Thoroughgood had something for him as he had something for Thoroughgood. Even though he doesn't know the content, he knows that Thoroughgood was killed to prevent it from being revealed. If he was to go to press with that story, it might be just enough to let us call in the cavalry and for Seth to come in from the cold. But for the moment all we can do is wait and pray.'

* * * * *

'The voice was not that of van Klaveren.'

Yat-sen was puzzled. If not van Klaveren, then who?

'Could it be, Tao, that you have acted precipitously in eliminating the journalist?'

'I do not understand, sir.'

'Your surveillance led you to believe that he was intending to communicate with another party over the public telephone system. We now know that this was not van Klaveren. Indeed, it is clear that there has been no telephone communication of any kind from the farmhouse. Our only indication that Thoroughgood was involved was an Internet search on his name by someone in the house. Killing the man might appear, to a disinterested party, as something of an overreaction, would you not agree?'

Tao was tired of the old man second guessing his actions. The kill was clean and the police were treating it as an accident. What if he had made a mistake? This man was of no consequence – was Yat-sen getting sentimental in his dotage?

'I am confident that this incident has not jeopardised our search for Whitten. I consider this a prudent precaution in the circumstances.'

'Do you indeed? I, on the other hand, consider your actions reckless; let us hope for both our sakes that it is you and not I who are correct. You must re-double your efforts Tao. Find out who this new voice belongs to. You must establish whether he is pertinent to our search for Whitten and this task must be accomplished without delay.'

Yat-sen hung up. Once again Tao's actions had been less than discreet. They were no nearer catching Whitten and a possible source of information had been snuffed out. Shanghai was getting impatient. The decision to eliminate Franks was clearly an error. Her methods, though too slow to apprehend Whitten, had been infinitely more successful than those of Tao. The time was not far away when the young man would be held to account for his failures. Yat-sen did not believe his career with the Tong would be a long one.

* * * * *

Seth was devastated. It had hardly been headline news. He had bought all the evening papers. Time was lying heavily on his hands and the boredom had lured him into the inside pages as he leafed through the various rags. It was not quite inside back page, but just 10 lines of a story and a page reference for an even shorter obituary.

Ye gods, how were they going to get out of this? Tao was sending a message that he meant business and that his reach was long. Randy and Connie must have been sloppy in their effort to get the story published. Anthony Thoroughgood would have been his journalist of choice and Connie would have known that. Now the only person at the BBC with the balls to publicly state a contrary argument to the received wisdom on global warming, was dead.

His attempt to simultaneously break the story of data fraud at the Page Climate Centre and Chinese mafia involvement in wind turbine manufacture had failed. Now they were just left fighting for their lives.

It had been in his mind for some days now; perhaps brought on by his epiphany, an angry reaction to the loss of all that he had held dear. It had just been a fantasy, the desire to destroy, to lash out at those who had perpetrated the global warming confidence trick on him for so many years. But as the failure of his plan started to sink in, the yearning to strike back had begun to grow and the seed of an idea, and how it could be accomplished, was beginning to take form.

What he needed was a spectacular, as the IRA used to call it. A headline-grabbing shocker. An explosion. And what better place to do it than at the jewel in the country's green energy crown, Whitelee in Scotland, Britain's largest onshore wind farm.

PART V

It is error alone which needs the support of gov-
ernment. Truth can stand by itself.

Thomas Jefferson

'Mr President, I have Ben Haze on the line for you.'

'Put him through.'

'Ben, long time, no hear.'

'I guess we have both been busy. Your first hundred days have been something of a baptism of fire.'

'Sure thing, but how goes the crusade?'

'Well, Mr President, that is why I have called. A recent incident in England has come to my attention that concerns me and I was wondering whether some discreet enquiries might be made to establish if there is anything that we need to worry about.'

'Tell me more.'

'Have you heard of a character called "Deep Cool"?'

'Can't say as I have, but go on.'

'This is the name given to an individual or individuals who have leaked a bunch of e-mails between the Page Climate Centre in England and members of the environmental community here in the States, including Professor Yat-sen.'

'Ah sure, Climategate, but hasn't that all died down now? Nobody's listening anymore.'

'I would have been inclined to agree but yesterday a British police officer investigating the source of those leaks was murdered inside a police station while in the process of interviewing two suspects, who are now missing. What is really interesting is the name of a third suspect who broke them out of jail – Jake Tao. We know this is an alias; we also know that this alias belongs to an enforcer with the Shanghai Tong.'

'Wait a moment, Ben. Should I be hearing any of this? I'm not sure I like the direction this conversation is going. What do you want from me?'

'Perhaps if I could brief one of your security chiefs and

see if there is anything that need concern us.'

'Sure thing, yes, do that. Keep me posted. Good talking to you. Now don't be a stranger.'

The line dropped. Haze stared at the phone. What had the Tong got to do with global warming sceptics and what were they doing breaking them out of a British police station? Climategate was dying a death; this incident was bound to breathe new life into it. Global warming was already skating on thin ice. None of the prophesied disaster scenarios were coming true. He had spent the past few years dodging the climate sceptics' demands for debate on the subject.

So much of the data on which he had based his global warming agenda for the election campaign had subsequently been shown to be suspect. His future shot at the presidency was reliant on the success of Green energy and especially carbon trading. Anything that might cast doubt on the veracity of human-induced global warming – the very pillar on which the BCX was built – threatened to undermine his ability to create the one-billion dollar campaign fund that would be needed to secure his elevation to the presidency and the guarantee of a Democratic successor to Asoka Mecheri.

The President's permission had given him free access to the vast United States data-gathering apparatus. This was a big plus and would enable him to get to the bottom of the incident. But there was a cloud on the horizon. The President had been short with him. Nothing overt but it seemed on reflection that the POTUS was trying to distance himself from any fallout from Climategate.

But the BCX was a joint venture; it was as much Mecheri's responsibility as it was his. Any investigation of the Climategate scandal was going to lead straight to Yat-sen *and any investigation into Yat-sen would lead to the President, carbon trading and the BCX. He needed to find out what was going on in England and put a lid on it. He pressed the intercom.*

'Janice, get me Henry at Langley. I need a chat.'

CHAPTER 22

It was late when Seth reached Cove Quarry, a small rocky outcrop about an hour south of Whitelee. He scanned the rubble strewn landscape and approach roads for any signs of life, but there was none. The track leading up to the rock face was muddy and the back end of the Jag slewed around as if it were on ice but he persevered. It was just the place to pick up the explosives he needed for his grand plan and quarries were notorious for their sloppy security.

His attention was grabbed by a rock drill poised to bring down the next strata of high grade metamorphic sandstone. Normally used for boring the holes down which sticks of dynamite were dropped prior to their detonation, it would become his high tech. battering ram. He hitched it to the Jag's tow bar and headed for the magazine, the car began slithering down the rough track and the rock drill following behind, bouncing from side to side like some demented Triffid.

Seth's plan was to drill out a square 3ft across so he could crawl into the quarries explosives magazine and get the dynamite he needed. He prayed the quarry men had left enough petrol in the rock drill's tank to get the job done.

He deployed the drill's four stabilisers as close to the magazine wall as he could get then set about starting the engine. Theoretically all you had to do was wind the crank handle until it fired. After five attempts, Seth's right shoulder and bicep were beginning to burn, then, oh joy of joys, the *put-put-put* as the engine burst into life.

Up to that point, Seth had not been too worried about the noise made by the engine, but once the drill encountered the brickwork, it was as if all hell had broken loose. As the hammer action kicked in, everything began to shake. Surely they would be able to hear this all the way to Glasgow, but if the impact of the drill on his hearing was like hell then the impact on the magazine was like heaven and within a few minutes he had freed a 3ft square block from the wall of the vault, giving him easy access to its most dangerous contents.

The dark interior of the brick tomb was dominated by a large green wooden box with a hinged lid. Next to the hole itself was something piled high with brick dust. Leaning in, Seth carefully lifted it out, tilting it as he did so to remove the enormous pile of debris. The blood drained from his face as he read the stark warning on the top of the box: 'Warning Detonators – Handle with extreme caution'. Approximately every 2 inches across the top of the box was a thin line tracing the track of the drill bit – 1 inch lower and the drill would have punctured the box and blown him to kingdom come.

Gingerly placing the box on the ground, he sat back as he began to shake violently. It was some moments before he was in any condition to lift the lid and review the contents: 100 cellophane-sheathed fuses with detonators attached.

He turned his attention to the large green box on the other side of the magazine. To retrieve it, Seth had to crawl in through the hole made by the rock drill. The box was almost full; he scooped up what was there and piled the brown-paper covered sticks onto the ground outside. Unlike the pristine detonators, the sticks of dynamite were old and sweating. A dark line ran the length of each stick; beads of nitro-glycerine had oozed out and trickled down to where they had been reabsorbed by the brown-paper wrapping. They were definitely coming to the end of their usable life.

He counted them – 100 half pound sticks, one for each of the detonators, 50lb of explosive. He had done his calculations with the aid of the US Army field manual which he had pulled off the web – God bless America's addiction to free speech – he needed 70lb to bring down a 350ft wind turbine. But the situation was not quite as bleak as it at first appeared. He had never meant to bring the tower down just by explosive power alone. He was intending to use the turbine against itself.

The three 20 ton propeller blades spun at 160 mph at full tilt. If a big enough shockwave could be driven up the tower and one of the blades touched it, explosives would not be required – you would need a brush and pan to sweep up the pieces.

But for now, he needed to get the explosives into the car and away from the quarry before anyone came snooping around. Seth piled the dynamite into the boot of the Jag. Although it had great suspension this was pretty much irrelevant as it was virtually impossible to ignite dynamite without a detonator. The detonators themselves were a different matter, these he gingerly placed in the middle of the back seat, fully belted in with extra padding provided by his sleeping bag.

He was all set to go when he remembered the detonator cord. It had to be in the magazine somewhere. Taking his torch from the car, he went back to make a thorough search. He quickly spotted a large reel hanging on the far wall. Hooking it down, he added it to his haul. He examined a carefully prepared list of supplies that he had gathered together to complete his bomb: flour, washing lines, cable ties, black tape, gaffer tape, refuse sacks, cigarette lighters – he had everything he needed except water, which he would pick up closer to his objective. He turned the Jag around and began the slippery assent up the track and out of the quarry to his final destination.

* * * * *

In London, Mates pored over every detail in the two brown envelopes. Whitten's figures showed that Chinese Iron and Steel alone stood to lose a turbine contract worth $24 billion with the British government if details of the pollution and corruption behind wind energy got out. The protagonists in this tale were part of a huge self-perpetuating cycle. Page Climate Centre reported increases in world temperatures, environmentalists clamoured for renewable energy, big business built wind turbines, China supplied rare earths for wind turbines – and paid Page to report increases in world temperatures and so it went round.

This was Pulitzer Prize material. It was also his death warrant if he did not handle it correctly. The three individuals who had put this together were living on borrowed time and they knew it. He and the late Anthony Thoroughgood were their lifelines. They were counting on him to give them such publicity that no one, not even the Chinese government, would dare to mess with them.

It was insufficient to print the story in the English papers; this stuff needed to be syndicated, not just in broadsheets, but on the web. He needed this to go viral and get the information out to as many people as possible to frustrate any attempts by vested interests to suppress it, and those vested interests were legion. Turbine manufacturers, power companies, politicians, research scientists, mining conglomerates, the list was endless. Hundreds of billions of dollars were at stake; reputations at the very top of governments worldwide were threatened. An entire belief system based on the premise that the burning of fossil fuels was heating up the planet to catastrophic levels was about to be brought crashing down.

* * * * *

Over the bleak horizon, the target of Seth's attack became visible. Even on the best of days, this was a desolate place. But it was this very desolation that drew the walker, the adventurer, to seek out unspoiled moorland, only to have their vision assaulted by an army of steel giants marching across a once pristine wilderness.

By now all the construction and tourist traffic had gone and he did not encounter a single car between the motorway and the large 'No Entry' signs that greeted him at the site entrance. He could not help but marvel at the engineering that had gone in to making this 'dark satanic mill'. He shuddered at the size of the dwarfing steel tower rising out of its massive concrete base.

The car was buffeted as he drove along the exposed ridge. The wind whistled around the window frames. He needed to get moving. The assembly time for the bomb was a completely unknown quantity. He accelerated down the track to the construction site office, which was surrounded by steel shuttering. Seth got out and almost had the door torn out of his grip by the force of the wind.

This was where he was counting on accessing the water he needed to focus the power of the blast. His luck was in. A large bore hose pipe lay at the locked gates and which, by dint of the piles of mud covering the surrounding area, was presumably used for washing off the lorry tyres before they went back on the public roads, all very environmentally friendly. He set about half filling the black plastic sacks with water. At a rough guess, he reckoned he was putting about 10 litres of water into each sack; any more than that and he would not be able to lift them into place and, anyway, they would probably tear.

He transferred the dynamite and the detonators onto the passenger seat and then began to distribute the water-filled sacks throughout the boot and back seat. He had folded over the top of the black sacks and then closed them off with a large cable tie, creating an effective watertight seal. By the time he had the last bag on board, the car's suspension was compressed to its maximum As the car pulled away, unpleasant grinding sounds could be heard from the rear as the tyres scraped against the inside of the wheel arches. Every minor bump in the road was rewarded with a metallic thump as the springs mashed together.

Seth drove very gently, as much for the protection of the detonators, which were now at his elbow, as for the weight of water which was destroying the cars suspension. He reversed as close as he could to the base of the nearest tower. His first job was to loop the washing line around the base. It was going to have to bear the strain of half a ton of water hanging from it. Four loops should do the trick. He was glad he had not skimped and had bought two reels. Standing on the boot of the car, he shimmied the loops of rope as far up the steel structure as he could, tying them off once they were at his maximum reach.

Next: the explosives. Sitting in the driver's seat with his feet hanging out of the door, the dynamite piled on the passenger seat and the box of detonators in the foot well, he began the delicate task of priming the explosives. Each stick of dynamite needed its own detonator. He inserted one into the paper-covered end of each stick. The explosive behaved like stiff putty and required some pressure to embed the detonator so that only the fuse cord protruded. Once each stick was finished, he laid it carefully on the sleeping bag that he had unrolled at his feet. After just 25 sticks, his fingers began to ache with the strain of inserting the thin silver rods.

When the hundredth stick lay piled on the ground, he swung his feet into the car, dropped the seat back and lay exhausted. As he massaged his hand and wrists to relieve the agony, he realised that, just like Don Quixote, he was tilting at windmills. He hoped he'd be more successful than the aged Spanish knight.

He divided the 100 sticks into bundles of five and taped them together with the fuses all pointing in the same direction and a 10ft length of detonator cord secured in the middle. The cut end nestled in the centre was guaranteed to ignite the surrounding detonator fuses once the cord was lit.

Seth taped the 20 mini bombs to the tower in two horizontal rows below the washing line. Each row was packed tightly together with the detonator cords hanging down beneath so that the flame of the fuse, once lit, travelled the same distance to each block of dynamite. Otherwise, the first sticks to explode would destroy the rest of the bomb before it had a chance to detonate.

His next task involved the bags of flour which, when agitated by the blast, would create a secondary explosion. Up to this point the whole device had looked elegantly destructive, like something assembled by Wile. E. Coyote in his never-ending attempts to bring about the demise of Road Runner. But with the flour bags attached, it looked messy with lines of tape going everywhere. 'Ah, what the hell!' Seth thought. 'It is all going to be covered up by the water bags anyway.'

Lifting up the first sack of water, Seth once again climbed on the boot of the car. Even with everything that was at stake, he still regretted the utter mess his shoes were making of the car's recent paint job. It was obvious he was not going to be able to get the first row of bags high enough from this vantage point. He climbed down and repositioned the car sideways on and this time climbed on the roof.

Using the bags' drawstrings, he tied a row of 12 to the bottom of the four washing lines, adjusting the height so that they completely covered the explosives. By the fourth row, his arms were killing him as he had to work for extended periods with his arms above his head. Once the last bag was in place, all the explosives were completely concealed and the tower looked as if someone had adorned it with several strings of large black beads.

Seth pulled the car a little way from the base

of the column giving him space to gather up the loose ends of the 20 detonator cords to which he would attach the final length of cord that would simultaneously detonate the 20 bomblets. They fluttered in the breeze, seeming to dance in time to the *whoosh-whoosh-whoosh* of the blades overhead, now spinning at their maximum speed – all the better for self-destruction.

Running the remaining cord back into the boot of the car, he was horrified when the end of the line detached from the spindle. What he had thought was at least another 20ft was just a large cardboard core. He could be no more than 15 feet away from the bomb, at a burn rate of 5ft per second that was not going to give him much time to get clear – but there was no going back now.

He tucked the loose end of the cord under his laptop and began setting up a satellite link. No doubt Tao was monitoring his sat. phone but by the time he was in any position to do something about it, the deed would be done and Deep Cool would be in the protective custody of the Glasgow police's armed response unit.

By now, the wind had reached such a pitch that it virtually drowned out the noise of the turbine. Among all the other things to worry about was the possibility that the wind would reach a speed that would trip the turbine's failsafe. If the blades stopped turning, the bomb would not be enough to bring down the tower.

Seth knew he'd have to work faster and get this over with before the wind did it for him. The internet link he was working on was essential. It would put Climategate once again at the top of the environmental debate and hopefully save Connie and himself from the clutches of the Tong.

CHAPTER 23

Sergeant Stuart had dedicated his professional life to this part of Scotland. In his early days as a policeman – some 30 years ago – it had been a poor corner of the British Isles. A little of the oil revenue of the 70s boom had trickled down from Aberdeen but not much. It was not until the noughties that things had really begun to look up with the building of Whitelee and the 'wind rush' that had brought in the money from construction and eco-tourism, that still continued apace.

As he drove along the high road from Kingswell to his home in Eaglesham, he enjoyed the view of the magnificent shining spires that dotted the landscape, pointing skywards like a victory salute. It was certainly an economic victory for his home town. His daughter worked in the visitor's centre and his wife ran a little shop selling all things green to the pilgrims who came from across Europe to see this testament to the success of alternative energy. Thanks to the environmental movement, life was good.

As he reached the brow of the hill, he spotted a red Jag parked by one of the spires in a restricted area. There was something odd about it. A large saloon, it was a bit long in the tooth and an unlikely mode of transport for the construction staff, who would normally have gone home by this hour. Although off duty, he decided to take a look. Pulling into the access road, he stopped about 10 yards from the car and walked over to the young man engrossed in something in the boot of the vehicle.

'All right, what do we have here, then?'

Seth's head shot up and, for the second time in a week, bashed off the boot lock. Stunned, he fell sideways to the ground. As he came to, he could feel a small trickle of blood running down his scalp. Looking up, his gaze was met by the furrowed brow and concerned expression of a ruddy-faced policeman.

'Sorry, son – didn't mean to startle you. Are you OK? Nasty cut you got there. You should get someone to take a look at that.'

Seth's mind raced. For a brief moment he considered rugby tackling the officer and tying him up while he finished the job. But the sight of the solid 6ft 2 inch frame of this burley Scotsman soon put paid to that idea.

'What are you doing here so late, lad – du ye have a problem?'

Seth's first utterance was a moan. Then he stood up and sat on the back bumper while he tried to decide what to do next.

'God, you put the heart across me. Can't hear a damn thing with this wind.'

'Ay, but what's your problem?'

'Just that – the damned wind. I'm with a team

from the turbine manufacturers.'

Fumbling in his pocket, Seth pulled out his student card, flashed it at Stuart and quickly put it back without allowing closer scrutiny.

'We discovered a crack at the base of this tower and with the wind forecast for tonight, we have to monitor it. I have rigged up a load of strain gauges along the crack – held in place by those water bags – and I'm monitoring them with my laptop. The readings are fascinating – do you want to take a look?'

Seth moved to one side and gestured towards the computer. Stuart's eyes followed the cable as it ran from the laptop and over the concrete to the base of the column. Technology had never been one of his fortes – his daughter had to help him retrieve his e-mails. He was a nuts and bolts man.

'No, you're all right. I need to be getting home – just wanted to make sure you were OK. Hope your tests work out.'

With that, he turned and walked back to his car. He came away deflated. This smart young man with his fancy car and all his tech talk; suddenly he felt old and in need of a dram.

* * * * *

Seth watched the policeman drive off. If he hadn't felt so utterly drained by the experience, he could almost have felt sorry for the man. When the bomb went off, the departing 'keeper of the peace' would probably be one of the first on the scene – how would he feel when he had been so close to the catch of his career? More to the point, how would he explain his failure to make the initial arrest to his bosses? Well, if he didn't mention it, neither would Seth. He owed him that at least for unwittingly letting him off the hook. This had been a hell of a wakeup call – he needed to get the job done.

Jumping into the car he strapped himself tightly into the seat belt and floored the accelerator making a bee line for the nearest ditch. The Jag left the road and dropped nose down stopping dead with a neck jarring thud. As he had calculated the boot with its securely attached tow bracket stuck proud above the level of the track. Extricating himself from the crashed vehicle he commenced work on establishing the uplink.

Within minutes everything was in place and with just one click the live feed would commence. Taking a roll of black tape, he began to attach a webcam to the tow hitch of the Jag. By the time he had finished, it was completely cocooned with only the lens and microphone visible. He was confident that it would remain attached after the explosion; in fact, he was counting on it.

Running the cable from the camera back down into the ditch, he plugged it into the USB port and checked the line-up on the tower – perfect. It was far enough away to capture the entire structure from top to bottom. The built in microphone was just able to pick up the sound of the blades over the distortion produced by the wind.

Grabbing a screenshot of the bomb-strapped tower, Seth emailed the picture to the news media websites and the Terrorist Reporting section of the Strathclyde Constabulary public system. Everything was set – it was time to put in the call.

'What service do you require?'

'Police.'

'What is the nature of the emergency?'

'I have planted a bomb at the Whitelee wind farm that will explode in the next few minutes.'

'Please state you name and current address.'

'Tell your boss to go onto the police website – I have left a picture of the bomb as proof of my bona-fides.'

'Could you spell that for me, sir?'

'If you want to have a job in the morning, I suggest you tell your boss three things: bomb, Whitelee, five minutes.'

* * * * *

'Sarge, we have just had a man on claiming to have planted a bomb at the Whitelee wind farm. He says he has left a picture of it on our website.'

'Not another loon – it's a bloody full moon, isn't it?'

'What should I do, sir?'

'Contact local uniform; see if they have any-one in the area.'

'Yes, sir.'

'Despatch – would you get an officer out to

Whitelee wind farm? We have a bomb threat and need a drive-by.'

* * * * *

Sergeant Stuart pulled up on the gravel verge opposite the Swan. With its faded green paint and feeble-looking pansies by the door, it attracted little passing trade but it had been his local for 30 years, as it had been for his father and a long line of Stuarts. It was a safe haven from the drudgery of domesticity – a place where he was well-known and welcome. Stepping through the door, he headed for the bar and his first drink of the evening – then his mobile went off.

'Chris, glad I caught you – I have a little job I would like you to do for me.'

'Fuck off! I've finished for the day.'

'Look, just do us a favour, will you? It won't take more than half an hour. Some crazy has just rung in claiming he's planted a bomb at Whitelee farm. I need you to run past it, just so we can say we've ticked the boxes.'

'Oh Jesus!'

'What?'

'I saw the bastard planting it – it's bloody huge! You'd better get the bomb squad down there – quick!'

* * * * *

Seth surveyed his work. The clock was ticking. The police would be on their way – hopefully. He ran a final test on the uplink then, taking out one of the cigarette lighters, he removed the plastic safety strip and flicked the knurled wheel a couple of times to check it was working. He paced out the distance from the end of the fuse cord to the edge of the ditch: 20 paces – 20 yards. At a sprint maybe 15 large strides. Holy shit, this was going to be close – he wasn't sure he was going to make it. He practised the dash a few more times. Each run was a fraction short but he counted on the adrenalin that would kick in once the fuse was lit to get him over the edge in time.

With the camera rolling, he strode out across the road in a manner he hoped was evocative of the famous scene from *High Noon*. Cupping his hands around the end of the fuse and lighter, he flicked the wheel and touched the madly dancing flame to the cord – it burst into life.

With legs at full stretch Seth bounded across the concrete. His peripheral vision greyed out, producing a tunnel effect with the focus sharply defined as the edge of the road. Nearing his goal, he made a swallow dive for the ditch and as he flew through the air he thought for a moment that the bomb had not gone off. It was as though a switch had been flicked in his head and someone had turned off his hearing. At that same instant the blast caught his exposed feet and flicked him head over heels.

* * * * *

Sergeant Stuart felt, rather than heard, the blast. He saw a column of smoke appear in the air above Whitelee. A large white object rose out of the cloud and described a lazy arc as it covered the 1 mile distance between the bombsite and Stuart's car in a little over 20 seconds. The aerodynamic shape gave it a grace that belied its destructive potential as it knifed into the road just 100 yards from the speeding Avensis.

The impact shattered the carbon fibre turbine blade into a thousand razor sharp shards that peppered the car's windshield and carpeted the road ahead with tyre-puncturing fragments. Stuart pulled the steering wheel hard to the left to avoid the protruding tip of the blade and, as he did so, the front tyres blew out as the side walls were shredded. The car careered off the road, slamming into a wall. Simultaneously the seatbelt tensioners fired as the airbags filled the car. Stuart was at once thrown forward then hauled back into his seat by the safety restraints.

For a few seconds he sat slumped over, then, as if on autopilot, he brushed away the deflated air bags, removed his seatbelt and opened the car door. As he stumbled out, he began a slow metronomic run towards the site of the explosion.

* * * * *

Seth landed hard on his back at the bottom of the ditch, knocking the wind out of him. Dust and debris rained down on his prone body. He felt as though someone had repeatedly punched him in the gut. His mouth was full of grit and his throat was scorched. Coughing and spluttering he rolled on his side, trying to get his wind back, and it took him several moments to recover himself.

Crawling to the top of the ditch, he rubbed his eyes, which had begun to water. Pulling a handkerchief out of his pocket, he started to clear his vision. As he peered through the dust and smoke, he felt his chest constrict when he saw the stump of turbine 012 poking out of the ground at a 45 degree angle.

The tower had been sheared in half; the top section lay to one side, the nacelle virtually intact with the stump of the rotor still attached. The high wind cleared the visibility in seconds giving the webcam a panoramic view of the destruction. Using the boot of the car to drag himself out of the ditch, Seth positioned himself so that the mayhem was in the background, and turning to the camera, he uttered the immortal words redolent of *Iron Man*.

'I am Deep Cool.'

CHAPTER 24

'In breaking news this evening, Deep Cool came in from the cold in spectacular fashion as he demolished a 400ft wind turbine at Europe's largest wind farm in Scotland, England.'

Connie stared at the CNN report in disbelief. There was Seth in front of the remains of a wind turbine, declaring to all the world that he was 'Deep Cool'. She didn't know what to make of the situation. Had he gone insane? She screamed for the others, who came running from various parts of the house. Rewinding the broadcast, Connie ran it again to the utter bemusement of all.

'Deep Cool has been identified as Seth Whitten, a 23-year-old graduate student at Norwich University from which the original Climategate e-mails were leaked. He is undergoing questioning by Strathclyde police in connection with an explosion, at 10 pm Greenwich Mean Time, which demolished a wind turbine and which was broadcast live on the worldwide web.'

'So this is the genius who has got us into all this mess, is it?' Cheryl glowered at Connie.

The two men exchanged furtive glances.

'What – what is it?' Cheryl looked panicked.

'Well, it's just that now Tao knows where Seth

is, we are no longer of any use to him. He could just let us be, but we know the background to his murder of Inspector Franks and he knows we have been in contact with journalists. The Tong are not going to want that to get out,' Ruairi chipped in.

'If he's going to make a move, he'll do it very quickly,' Randolph added. 'We need to get out of here now. Do you have anything faster than that jalopy of a Land Rover of yours, Ruairi?'

'No, but even if we had, they will have the farm covered by snipers; we would never make it to the barn.'

At this news, Cheryl stared at Ruairi in disbelief. He put his large arms around her and hugged her close.

'Look, Ruairi, there must be something we can do. Do you have any weapons?'

'A couple of shotguns in the barn. But I have a better idea.'

* * * * *

Yat-sen touched the button on his phone.

'You have news for me, Tao?'

'Yes, Professor. Whitten has given himself up to the police in Scotland.'

'Surely this is not what you have telephoned to tell me? Everyone who cares to listen knows this. The world's media have been alerted to the situation. What are we to do, Tao?'

'I propose that we move swiftly and eliminate

him while he is still in the custody of the British authorities.'

'You disappoint me, Tao. This is not the kind of thinking that will help us. I believe that course of action would cause an international incident and this is something that our masters in Shanghai would not thank us for. It is also my belief that he will have informed his captors of our intent and they will have effected significant security precautions that even you, Tao, would be unable to penetrate.'

'Then what course of action do you propose, O Great One?'

This insult did not go unnoticed. The young assassin's days with the organisation were numbered. Yat-sen decided to let the slight pass; he still needed Tao's expertise.

'You are to move in on the farm. Take the girl and kill the others. Let it be known that we have her. Make sure that information gets to Whitten. This is how we will silence him.'

This would be Tao's last assignment. Yat-sen placed the call to Shanghai. It would be a difficult conversation; he would request Tao's recall. The specialist would be sacrificed; this is how he would save his own skin.

* * * * *

Jack Mates' editor had resorted to sending messenger boys to ring his doorbell. The *Daily Mail* was out of contact with its lead investigative reporter. There was no response from his mobile or land line. No one had seen him – it was as if he had dropped off the face of the earth.

'What the hell is that old bastard up to? He sends me a cryptic message that he has the scoop of the century, then nothing. Not even a postcard. If we have not heard from him by midnight, we are going to press without him. WHERE THE FUCK'S MY COFFEE?'

Maurice Zimmerman was up to 90. His best investigative reporter, and oldest friend, had asked him to hold the front page. He had worked with Jack on and off for almost 30 years and not once had he ever asked him to do that. It was too melo-dramatic – not like Jack at all. His recent behaviour led him to believe that something big was afoot, either that, or Jack was having a breakdown. It was 11.30 pm. Copy had to be filed by midnight at the latest if they were to have any chance of meeting the 4 am shipping deadline.

'If we don't hear from him in 30 minutes, we go with the "Deep Cool" kid and the windmill. Do we have a headline for that piece yet?'

Each night this close to the midnight cut-off, Zimmerman resorted to communicating with his staff simultaneously by bellowing through his open office door. At 11.55 pm, a shout went up from the floor.

'Jack's piece is in.'

'Send it through to me. This better be good, that's all I can say.'

The first thing that was wrong was that it was long, far too long. What the hell was he playing at? This was a newspaper, not a bookshop. He looked again at the page count – 30 pages. What the fuck! He didn't have time to read all this.

'Stella, Stella, get in here. You take the back half of Jack's piece; read the last 15 pages for me, will you?'

'Yes, boss.'

His heart began to sink. He couldn't run this – it read like a spy novel. There was no time to verify the claims. If it was true, it would have implications across the globe. It would be the biggest story of his career. But what if it wasn't true, or parts of it weren't true? He didn't want a 'Hitler Diaries' debacle on his hands. That had cost the *Sunday Times* editor his job.

'No, forget it, Stella. We can't go with this. Run the windmill thing.'

'But, boss, this *is* the windmill thing. They killed Franks.'

'Who did?'

'The Chinese mafia. She was hunting "Deep Cool". It all adds up. They also killed Anthony Thoroughgood.'

'Who the hell is he?'

'You know the BBC environmental correspondent – died in a hit and run yesterday in Leeds? He was on his way to meet Jack with the other half of the story. I tell you, it's all true. You have to run this, boss!'

* * * * *

'Follow me and keep your heads down. Don't go near the windows.'

Ruairi dodged out of the lounge bent double and ran to the downstairs bathroom. Flinging open the door, he got down on his hands and knees and prised up one of the small floor tiles with his fingers. Underneath was a large metal ring. He gave it a pull and a section of the bathroom floor came away.

'Randy, grab a load of coats from the closet. It's cold down there and we might be stuck in this place for a while.'

Ruairi pushed the floor panel to one side, revealing a short flight of near vertical stone steps. Cheryl went first closely followed by Connie and Randy with his bundle of coats. Just as Ruairi closed the bathroom door, he heard a tinkle of breaking glass, then a cacophonous boom that shook the house. Placing the lose tile back over the metal ring he followed the rest of the group down the steps before quickly sliding the panel back into place. It dropped with a heavy thud, just as another explosion rocked the house.

'They're using flashbangs,' whispered Ruairi. 'They obviously want to take us alive.'

The four fugitives huddled together at the back of the tiny cave. 'Don't put any light on and don't move. There is a well over to the right – we don't want anyone falling down it.'

The cellar was part natural, part manmade. Its

290

soft limestone bedrock eaten away by rainwater, it was one of tens of thousands of caves that riddled the Nottinghamshire countryside, giving the area the record for the most manmade caves anywhere in Europe.

After the first two explosions, little could be heard from above. Ten minutes went by before Connie piped up.

'Do you think they've gone?'

'Keep your voice down. No, I'm sure they're searching the place. Now – no noise, no light. Quiet, capiche?'

The walls of the cave were smooth from the action of running water. There was a not unpleasant damp smell. The air was surprisingly fresh. In the dark, Randolph had distributed the coats out to the other three. He had no idea whether they were men's or women's, but they kept them off the cold stone floor.

* * * * *

The radio in the van crackled into life.

'There's no sign of them. We have searched the place from top to bottom – they must have escaped.'

'Not possible, they must be still in there.'

Tao was frantic. His reputation was already in the mud. If he failed to deliver the girl, his life was over.

'Burn it down.'

'But the girl, you said we were to take her alive?'

'Burn it down, the smoke will drive them out like the cockroaches they are. Make sure they do not get away.'

CHAPTER 25

'**D**o you smell that?'

'Oh Jesus, it's smoke.'

'They've set fire to the farm; they're trying to smoke us out.'

'No, no,' Cheryl began to wail.

Ruairi quickly put his hand over her mouth and hugged her close.

'Shush shush. There's nothing we can do.'

All Cheryl could think about was their personal possessions; everything that they had collected over a lifetime together. The photos of the children when they were small, the videos, everything destroyed and all because of that bastard boyfriend. Her emotions seesawed between rage and despair. If she ever got her hands on him, she would wring his neck.

Randolph's imagination began to run riot. Visions of the cellars under Dresden after the city was firebombed at the end of World War II flashed before his eyes. When rescuers opened up the shelters, all the occupants were dead. Untouched by the firestorm, they had died from suffocation when all the oxygen had been sucked out of their refuge by the raging inferno. Was this to be their fate?

Randolph pulled his coat tighter round him to counter the chill. Was that a breeze? There was a slight hissing noise, like gas escaping, which seemed to be coming from the cellar door. Very soon the crackling of burning timbers could be heard from above and a strange creaking sound as though someone was trying to lift the cellar door.

It was soon apparent that the heat of the fire was sucking the air out of the cave, causing the cellar door to flutter up and then fall back down again as the pressure was equalised. The fire was being fed by the air in the cave network and due to the funnel effect, it was keeping the occupants sufficiently supplied with oxygen but it was also causing the fire to burn more intensely. Their terror rose as they began to feel the heat radiating down from the trap door. It would not be long now before the door burned through and they were all incinerated.

With an almighty crash, the gable wall of the house came tumbling down, bringing the roof timbers with it and showering flaming wreckage into the bathroom, filling the cramped surroundings in the cellar with dust and splinters of wood. The two women screamed as the wooden frame, which was all that stood between them and oblivion, sagged under the weight of the rubble. They were trapped.

* * * * *

'We did not see anyone exit the building. It would

appear that they have chosen to die in the fire rather than die at the hands of our marksmen.'

'This cannot be true, Tao. You tell me that you burned down the dwelling and that the fire officers are carrying away four bodies. Did you confirm that the girl is among them?'

'The light is fading, Master. There are many police at the scene – it would be risky to approach.'

'We need to know if the girl is indeed dead. If so, our ability to control Whitten is at an end and you and I, Tao, are also at an end. You need to be sure.'

* * * * *

As the fire engine barrelled down the small country lane leading to the farm, the omens did not look good. The property was totally engulfed in flame and anyone left inside was a goner. A single vehicle stood in the yard, paint blistered down one side from the heat of the burning building. There was no one in sight.

'Could be bodies, lads – keep an eye out.'

The Captain's warning to his crew was received with sombre nods of the head. Piling out of the tender, they were soon joined by the other unit and, within seconds, four hoses were pummelling the building. The upper story had gone and anyone who had been unfortunate enough to be trapped inside would now be somewhere at ground level. The Captain leaned his head into his lapel mike and squawked the station.

'Need a couple of ambulances out here, probable casualties. Tell them no need to hurry.'

'Understood.'

With just one hose still damping down, the men began to pick their way through what was left of the house. The blaze had been intense and Captain Matkin was beginning to have his suspicions. Clearly the fire had started at the back door and spread rapidly. The tell-tale signs of accelerant use were everywhere in the hallway. Once again he fingered the button on his mike.

'Need Forensics out here – looks like arson.'

Brushing aside the fallen timbers, he worked his way through to the centre of the building. His boots squelched in the black sludge generated by the combination of charcoal and water. Standing by what remained of an internal door frame and looking into what had once been a bathroom, a slight vibration trembled through his boots, a thump. There it was again.

He bent down and knelt on the shattered floor tiles, pushing aside a large beam and lifting a lump of masonry out of the way. He exposed what appeared to be a charred hole in the floor. Putting both hands on the ground, he leaned forward to get a better look when a hand shot out from the hole grabbing him by the collar, pulling him face first into the dirt, the visor of his helmet becoming jammed flat against the tiles.

'Listen to me.'

Panic welled up in his throat as he tried in

vain to break the grip of this manic troglodyte.

'There are people out there with rifles trained on you and your men. If they find out we are alive, all of us are dead. Do you understand? DO YOU UNDERSTAND?'

'Yes, I get it – let go of my neck.'

'Call your men over; tell them you have found four bodies. Do not let on we are alive.'

The grip on his throat relaxed and he quickly pulled away, falling back into a sitting position not quite believing what he had just heard. But there was something about the power in the voice, it was forceful, almost military. He staggered back out of the room and called over to his nearest officer.

'Go fetch me some cutters. I think I've found something.'

He did not want to alert the rest of the crew. He couldn't tell them the mad story he had just heard. It was surreal. Did he think what just happened actually happened? He took off his helmet and went back to the hole.

Putting his mouth to the ground he shouted down, 'Stand back; we will have you out of there soon.'

The voice hissed back, 'Shut the fuck up! Get four body bags and when the ambulance arrives, load us in as corpses. They must not know we are alive. They will be watching.'

'Come on, mate, you have got to give me more than that. This is crazy talk.'

Randolph thought for a moment.

'OK then, my friend and I are from Norwich.

We were in the police station when the officer was shot dead last week. The guy that did it is the one who lobbed grenades into this house and burned it down. He is also the one who has a bead on your head and who will kill you if you let on there are survivors.'

'Look, I guessed that this was arson and the police will be here soon, so can we lose the James Bond act?'

'You don't get it, do you? Unless your bobbies are from the SAS, they are going to last about two minutes. Humour me. What's the worst that could happen? If I'm wrong, you look like a dick and your mates will rib you 'til the end of time. If I'm right and you don't play along, then we all go out of here in body bags. The choice is easy. Now go get those fucking bags.'

* * * * *

Tao walked back down the road to the junction of Rickets Lane. The tears began to flow. He could see the headlights of the ambulance in the distance driving towards him. He stood in the road frantically waving his arms. The ambulance with nowhere to go slowed down and stopped. Seeing the man in such distress, the driver wound down the window.

'What's wrong, son?'

'My sister, they say she was in the fire. Please tell me she was not in the fire.'

'I'm sorry, son, I can't give out any information on identities.'

'But was there a girl – did a girl get out alive?'

'I shouldn't be telling you this, but four people died in that fire. Two of them were women – I'm so sorry.'

Tao moved away and the ambulance drove on. He composed himself. The crocodile tears had come easily, too easily. Life as he knew it was over. He looked back at the van, turned and began walking – in the opposite direction.

* * * * *

'You can come out now, he's gone. I'm reasonably sure that was Tao from what I remember of his picture from the Norwich CCTV. Didn't look like an international assassin but then who can tell?'

The police officer was dressed in a borrowed paramedic's uniform and bulged out of the tight-fitting garments. He pulled out his radio and contacted the armed response unit heading up from Nottingham

'… Asian, male, 6 ft, walking in your direction, armed and extremely dangerous. Careful with this one, guys. He won't come easily.'

The nurse in the back of the ambulance un-zipped the body bags and the four 'corpses' sat up. While not burned, there was no doubting that they had been in a fire. Each one had a head of grey hair courtesy of the fine ash that had penetrated their bolt hole. The women's faces were tear-streaked and their clothes caked with dried sludge from the hosing down the burnt out farm had received.

Connie and Cheryl sat up and hugged each other. It was the first bit of warmth either had shown since their original meeting two days ago. Surviving adversity can have a strange effect on people, Randolph thought. They sat in silence as the vehicle headed towards Robin Hood airport and their flight to London and protective custody.

CHAPTER 26

The journey from Scotland had not been a pleasant one. The local police did not react kindly to the presence of a 'terrorist' on their patch, particularly Sergeant Stuart, who had taken the near miss with a turbine blade rather personally. He needed to be physically restrained by his colleagues when he finally arrived at the explosion site, sweating and dazed but still up for laying Seth out, if he was given half a chance. No amount of protestations would convince Stuart that Seth had not aimed the blade at him deliberately.

For Seth, being trussed up and sandwiched between two heavily armed officers was, on the one hand comforting, while on the other, physically uncomfortable. His detailed knowledge of the identities of two of the three suspects in the murder of Inspector Franks had gained him serious credibility at the highest level. While not garnering sympathy for his cause, it had persuaded senior Strathclyde officers that there was more to Seth's story than met the eye.

The Met. wanted him immediately in relation to the murder of one of their own and this trumped the Scots' demand that they hold him for putting one of their shiny new wind machines out of action. The three-van police convoy to Prestwick airport bore testimony to the Met's belief that he was a marked man and would not last the night if not heavily protected.

To Seth's surprise, the convoy did not stop at the airport terminal building but drove through security gates and onto the concrete apron towards the lights of an open hangar, in front of which lurked the dark silhouette of a helicopter. Truly, they were not taking any chances with him.

The vans stopped just a short distance from the swirling blades and the last few feet of his journey on Scottish soil was flanked by six men clutching assault rifles. Seth did not feel that he had been that persuasive when he had informed his interrogators about his mortal danger. Something else must have happened to have initiated such a significant response. His level of anxiety rose and his mood darkened.

He was joined in the helicopter by two of his honour guard as well as his two minders from the van. The four sat in silence as the whine of the rotor blades increased and the chopper lifted off the ground. It was going to be a long journey. The lights of the airport quickly faded into the night as they rapidly moved out over dark open country.

* * * * *

Connie had managed to snatch a few minutes'

sleep on the flight down. It was well after midnight before the four bedraggled travellers were eventually accommodated in cells beneath the offices of New Scotland Yard. Their clothes were sent off to the laundry and they were kitted out with white coveralls and disposable underwear but by far the most satisfying comfort afforded the group was the opportunity to have a hot shower. The facilities were basic but felt luxurious after hours spent caked in grime and stinking of smoke and stale sweat.

When they reunited, it was in a corridor flanked by cell doors. Four of them were open and left that way. Even so, there was no exit as the corridor was closed off by heavy steel gates at both ends, but at least they could walk around, not that anyone wanted to. They took to their individual cots with not much more than a nod of acknowledgement that they had all survived the night and they would see what the next day would bring.

Breakfast came early, at 7 am. Their debrief and interrogation was due to begin at 8 am. Representatives from MI6 counter terrorism would sit in as observers. The interviews would be conducted individually, no doubt to check the stories all matched up.

Connie was led away first and shown into a large board room where three men sat with their backs to her as she entered. Their attention was focused on the large TV screen at the far end of the room. The breathless reporter was detailing the links between the Page Climate Unit and Professor

Jiang Yat-sen. How the Chinese government had secretly funded the keeper of the world's temperature via Yat-sen and how he was accused of falsifying the Chinese temperature record for the last 60 years. The ticker was linking Franks' death with the Tong, Yat-sen and Deep Cool.

As Connie stared at the screen, a familiar face turned around to see who had entered the room. Their eyes locked and tears flowed. Seth flung back his chair and took off across the room, knocking the wind out of her as he lifted Connie off the ground and swung her around in a fierce bear hug.

'Put me down, put me down – I can't breathe.'

Reluctantly he lowered her to the floor and they kissed as if to draw the very stuff of life from each other's bodies. No other words passed between them. They seemed exhausted by the passion of the moment. The others in the room took in the very public display of affection with not much more than a wry smile. There was a lot of work to get through and it was not going to get done with a whole lot of emotion in the way.

Seth spoke first. 'How did you get the story out? I thought Thoroughgood was dead.'

'He is, but we sent the information to a second journalist, who we also thought was a goner – I don't know how, but he put it all together and broke the story this morning. Oh God, so many times since you disappeared, I thought you were dead.'

She broke down – cradled in his arms. The

attending security personnel were now starting to lose patience.

'OK people, now, can we get down to business?'

Epilogue

It was his Chappaquiddick moment. As the news spread around the world, the price of carbon began to fall. That morning it had been trading at $7 a ton. By day's end, it was 10 cents. Haze had been heavily leveraged. His losses ran into hundreds of millions. All hopes of a political comeback were dashed.

The whiskey tumbler slipped from the puppet master's fingers and fell with a thud onto the thick carpet. He opened his jaw wide so as not to knock the cold steel off his teeth. When the barrel touched the back of his mouth, he pulled the trigger.

* * * * *

'And finally in late breaking news – the alleged murderer of Detective Inspector Franks of the metropolitan police has been captured after a gun battle in Sherwood Forest. A badly wounded man was taken under armed guard to Nottingham Royal Infirmary where his injuries are said not to be life threatening.

'In a related story Seth Whitten and Constance Bennett have been reunited after the self-confessed bomber of the Whitelee wind farm was released on bail pending his trial later this year. In defence of his actions he told reporters out-

side the Old Bailey, "It is the wind energy advocates that should be on trial, not me".'

* * * * *

'Mr President, the press are asking for a comment on claims that the death of ex-vice President Haze is linked to the collapse of the BCX and the resignation and indictment of Professor Yat-sen...'

Afterword

To Kill an Error is an attempt to popularise the sceptic view of human caused global warming and asks the reader to question commonly held beliefs about one of the most contentious issue of modern times.

While the author's scepticism about the long-term commercial viability of wind energy goes back almost 40 years, the bulk of his research has taken place in the last four years. Although the book is fiction the factual elements are largely based on the public stances taken by both sides of the global warming debate.

Acknowledgements

I would like to thank:
- Tess Tattersall – Editor
- Kieran Kelly – Legal Editor
- Dr. John J Ray whose blog has sustained me through these long years of research
- John S. – contributor to Climate Audit, for the 'Deep Cool' moniker
- My family, for never letting me believe too much.